# The Diary in the Old Valentine Box

## By

## Linda Salinas

This book is a work of fiction. Names, characters, establishment, organizations, and incidents are either products of the author's imagination or used factiously to give a sense of authenticity. Any resemblance to actual persons living or dead, events, or locales is entirely coincidental.

ISBN-13: 9781790775613

*In Memory*

*Pat Romachek*

# Acknowledgments

Writing this book has been a fourteen-year journey. Although I started the story shortly after retiring from the Highland Park Independent School district in 2004, it was a start and stop process that depended on vacation time. I could never tear myself away from daily activities long enough to ever finish it. I found that during vacation time, and when away from home, I could focus and write. I actually completed the book while on vacation in Cabo San Lucas, Mexico. Pat Romachek and wife Patty Rees invited us on two occasions to join them in their beautiful home on the side of a mountain overlooking the ocean. While they took my husband Albert golfing, I had complete quiet time in the most wonderful setting to finish my story. Still, that was almost two years ago, and I doubt seriously I would have ever taken the steps to actually publish it had it not been for a tragedy that happened on the first day of November 2018. Pat was killed in a motorcycle accident and Patty was very seriously injured. Finishing this book was important to me so that I could dedicate the book in Pat's memory. Pat, we miss you but feel blessed to have had time to spend with you. We will see you again. Save us a place.

I am also blessed to have a wonderful husband, Albert Salinas and a beautiful daughter and her husband, Carla and Joe Pickrel. I have the best mother anyone could have, Joyce Johnson; sister Brenda and her husband Thom, and son Alek; sister-in-law Tracy and sons Marc and Eric. I'm blessed with the Salinas family that I have been a part of for the last 30 years. I'm truly blessed.

## Chapter One
Summersong Lane
February 2001

The old, dilapidated house stood at the far end of a pretty, tree-lined street and adjacent to a wooded area that would remain undeveloped for many years to come.  It was the last house on Summersong Lane, so most townspeople never drove by it, and it had been forgotten for almost 15 years.  From the backyard, a solitary mountain could be seen in the distance.  The mountain was a silent giant, looming up into the heavens, hiding the beautiful valley that lay at its feet.  The mountain wasn't even noticed by the townspeople who saw it every day. It was like the sunsets in Arizona or the ocean on the coast. People overlook beautiful scenery when they live daily in its presence.  The townspeople scurried around town, darting in and out of shops without ever looking up in its direction. To visitors, it was absolutely beautiful---reaching high into the sky, carpeted with lush green trees and thick shrubs. Sometimes heavy, dark clouds hid the very top, making one wonder just how high the mountain actually reached.  It made a picturesque backdrop to the small, quaint town that lay only a few miles away.

The small house at 1313 Summersong Lane had remained vacant since 1986---almost fifteen years.

The paint on the clapboard exterior was faded and cracked. A few shingles had blown off during the spring thunderstorms and more than one shutter had come off one of the hinges, causing it to hang at an awkward angle and sway in the wind. The floorboards were broken on the front porch, making a dangerous walk for anyone wanting to venture up to the front door. The green lawn had long ago disappeared and was replaced by bare, dry ground and a few unwelcoming weeds. No one seemed to mind that the house was slowly dying. Then one day, a "For Sale" sign went up near the sidewalk close to the road.

John and Diane Johnson were not unlike many other young, married couples. They saved every penny they could save to buy a house to call their own. They did little, odd jobs for people in the community and never touched the earnings no matter how tempted they were to do so. Diane refrained from walking into the local dime store for fear that she would find something she really wanted. She wanted to avoid asking herself the question, *Should I spend $.30 for that spool of hair ribbon? Can I live without it for now?* Invariably, she always answered herself the same way----*Yes, I can live without it for now. I will buy it someday--- later.* John and Diane had a goal in mind and nothing would keep them from reaching it.

Married for only three years, they wanted to get into a house they could afford and fix it up in anticipation of beginning a family. John came from a large family and sharing a bedroom with one or two siblings was no big deal---in fact, it was expected. Diane was from a small family –only two children—and she had a bedroom of her own from the very beginning. The little house on Summersong was the perfect size for their needs.

John worked at the local lumberyard that his uncle owned. He actually started on a part-time basis while still in high school. The extra money that he earned enabled him to fix up his car---not to 'supe' up the engine or put a shiny, new paint job on it--- but just to fix it up to keep it running. With parents of very modest means, the kids had to find odd jobs to pay for any of the extras they wanted. Having a car in the first place was pretty special but it had actually been a hand-me-down from one of his uncles. The car managed to keep going through several of his cousins' ownership before landing at his feet. John's job at the lumberyard paid for his oil, gas, and minor repairs. He was quite appreciative that his brothers and cousins had been pretty talented when it came to repairing old cars.

John was tall and muscular and was able to build anything that he saw. He was a handyman and could fix plumbing and electrical problems fairly easily, also. That is one reason Diane was not disturbed by the condition of the house. She had all the confidence in the world in John's abilities. She had seen his work. Throughout the years, she observed him replace the electrical fuse box in his parent's garage, find the short in the attic light, and add a ceiling fan in the living room. He fixed the leaking plumbing in the bathroom and replaced the faucets in the kitchen. And when his mother wanted a new cabinet added in the kitchen, he built it to perfection. It matched the existing cabinets perfectly. In Diane's eyes, John could do anything.

When John wasn't working at the lumberyard, he did odd jobs for some of the townspeople. Having gained quite a reputation for building things with wood, he was called upon to build cabinets, bookshelves, simple pieces of furniture, and fences. He managed to get quite a bit of building projects done in his spare time. He saved every dime. It seemed that the townspeople knew he was a hard-working young man with a goal and they were more than obliged to help him out.

Diane was equally as talented but her talent was mostly artistic. She could draw and paint and was a great seamstress. She learned how to sew from her mother who once owned her own drapery business. Diane loved making curtains and draperies when she was not working at the Prestonwood Elementary School. She was a secretary in the principal's office and was quite busy except in the summer when she had several weeks off for summer vacation. That break was her time to fix up her home and putter in the yard. Often, Diane found herself overwhelmed with sewing projects from parents and teachers at the school. She also had a job wrapping presents at the local department store over the Christmas holidays. She was fast and the gifts turned out beautifully, so she made quite a bit of loose change in just a few days' time. Diane wasn't opposed to "ironing for hire" either, although it wasn't a job that she enjoyed. Babysitting was a natural for Diane. She was excellent with children and they loved staying with

"Miss Diane." So, between the two of them, they were saving quite a bit---all in preparation of getting their own home.

John and Diane were amazed at how their little nest egg grew. Yes, they gave up a lot of their free time or leisure time but they were both young and could easily handle it. They still had plenty of time to do things they wanted to do. It was particularly nice when they could work on projects together or at least be together while working on their separate projects. Once, John built a cornice board while Diane sewed the fabric to cover it. They both installed the new window dressing in Mrs. Judd's house with pride. She praised and praised the work they had done. "I am so happy with your work that I am going to pay you more! Here is another little bit for your house fund!" John and Diane glowed.

John and Diane had been living in a small, one-room efficiency in the back of her parents' home. They were allowed to live there free of rent, and only had to pay the electric bill. This enabled them to save money for *their* first home. They took very good care of the little house and cared for their section of the yard perfectly. Diane was great with flowers of all kinds and always had a large pot of periwinkles nestled by their front door.

They were also more than frugal with their use of electricity. Lights were not turned on unless absolutely necessary. Their little heater was turned off even on the cold nights because they could cuddle up under several of the family's heirloom quilts. Diane still remembered walking into the room where her grandmother was having the "quilting party." Diane always wondered what they meant by "quilting party." Well, maybe it was a party since all the ladies seemed to be having such a great time! A large quilt was held horizontal by a wood and metal quilting frame. The ladies, sitting in chairs all the way around the quilt, were sewing designs onto the quilt so that the padding turned out beautifully. I bet there was a lot of gossiping going on at that quilting party! Every winter when Diane pulled out the quilts, she could see her grandmother and all of her grandmother's friends laughing and talking while sewing needles maneuvered between their fingers. And, if those little, old ladies knew what comfort those quilts provided, they would be so proud!

The little, three-bedroom cottage would be ideal, if they could manage all of the repairs that would have to be done to make it livable. Although it sat vacant and in ruins for many years, there was still a lot of personality that was just begging to be realized. It was as if the house had a spirit of its own, asking to be rejuvenated by a young family who could really care about it. Some townspeople claimed it was haunted and that the ghosts of the previous occupants often came to visit the old homestead. Others knew ghosts weren't real and would hear nothing of the idea but still wondered who occasionally put flowers in the old, stone vase on the side fence---children perhaps—on their way home from school. It could also be the old lady who walks in the neighborhood. No one really knew but fresh-cut garden flowers appeared in the stone vase from time to time.

2

"John!" Diane said as they approached the dilapidated, old cottage. "I think we can do something with this! All it needs is a little fixin' up."

"A little?" John answered, somewhat sarcastically and already knowing the answer to his question. "I can see six months of work just getting the yard in front of the house presentable. Heavens knows what the inside looks like! I'm almost afraid to go in!"

As they stood staring at the house, they could feel the gentle breeze of the wind as it rustled the wildflowers and caused the real estate sign to sway. Small chains holding up the small sign with the agent's phone number slightly creaked as though to tell the young couple to make the call. Reluctantly, John wrote the number on the back of a bank deposit slip. At the same time, he thought how they had saved over the past three years and deposited their savings into a special account, ---and for what, this house? Every nickel and dime of spare change went into a special jar that they referred to as their 'house jar' since the savings would be for their house. John just wasn't too sure about the whole idea. Diane didn't seem to even flinch at the idea of buying this old house. In fact, her eyes seemed to sparkle as she looked at it.

"Johnny, can't you see? We could tear up this old, cracked sidewalk and actually lay a little, cobblestone pathway to the front door! I've seen it in the decorating books. You plant tiny mosses in between the stones for a beautiful, carpeted effect. The little picket fence could be repaired and painted and it will look just like something from the Home and Gardens magazine! I know it doesn't look like anything now, but I can see it in my mind--- I can see what it can become!" Diane was glowing as she talked about possibilities for the old house and yard. Her eyes sparkled and seemed to dance just thinking about it. Diane could see into the future. She didn't see the old, dilapidated house---she saw a beautiful, white cottage with green shutters and a small, picket fence. She didn't see the grassless, weed-infested yard. She saw a lush lawn bordered by colorful flowers and divided by a quaint, stone walkway.

"Well, you've always seen the good in everything run down and ugly. You saw something in me, didn't ya?" Playfully, John grabbed Diane around her waist and spun her around. Laughing, they almost fell to the ground. "OK, Sweetie, but just don't get your heart set on this house 'til we've seen the inside. There's probably a reason this house has been vacant for so long!"

The windows had been boarded up long ago. Glass windows were tempting targets for the neighborhood boys who took great pride in being able to knock them out from the edge of the street. Officer Smith followed up with every lead he ever had on the vandalism and probably knew who had taken part but decided that boarding up the windows would allow him time to spend on more important matters---like teenagers drag racing down Main Street at 2:00am or following up on the building materials that were reported stolen from the new daycare center being built near the elementary school.  Late on Fridays, he usually had the drunken, construction workers from the nearby town of Cedar Mills.  He could never quite figure out why they always wanted to come to his small town to get boozed up—except that Miss May fed them one of the best home-cooked meals to be found anywhere and she always had a whole flock of pretty, little, young ladies who were always hanging around to enjoy the company of the men, once they were all cleaned up and sweet smellin'.  Miss May sort of ran a homemade-matchmaking service and was proud of the fact that several marriages came out of her efforts over the years.

"See there, in that white house on the corner?"  Miss May would say, "That sweet Angela married Jonathan Black last year.  She was one of the best waitresses I ever had in my place and she met Jonathan when he came in with a group of workers one Saturday.  When he said he wanted some 'take-out', I thought he meant 'food'."  Dying laughing and buckling over at the waist, she continued, "He meant he wanted to take Angela out! Long story short----too late----they started goin' out and he married her a year later!  Well, I lost me a good girl---sure did."  Miss May had a million stories like that, having had the kitchen more than thirty years.

John followed up with the phone call to the

15

real estate agent and set up an appointment to meet to see the house. He and Diane were going to meet the realtor at 10:30 the next morning--an elderly gentleman well known in the community. They got to the house a few minutes early to glance at the backyard before the agent arrived. Hearing his car door shut at the front of the house, they scurried around the corner to greet him.

"You must be the Graves," the white-haired gentleman said as he walked up the cracked and uneven sidewalk to the front porch. "I'm Tom Ridnour and more than happy to take you on a tour of this fine abode." Everyone laughed knowing that the shape that the house was in could be described as anything BUT a fine abode.

Tom had lived in Slaton since he was a young child. He literally watched the town grow from a small, single-street town to the bustling community that it had become. He started in the real estate business while in his early thirties so he had seniority over everyone in his office. He also knew every piece of property that ever hit the market. Now that he was older, he had slowed down a bit. He only went to the office when he really felt like it, and constantly handed off his listings to the younger crowd in the office. He felt they needed the business more than he did. He was also proud of the fact that he was the town's walking encyclopedia of information on the community people. He knew almost everyone by name, whom their parents were, whom they married, and how many children they had. Anytime anyone wanted to know the background of a person, they'd give ol' Tom a call.

"No, actually," Tom went on to say, "This house has seen better days, of course, but you look just like the type of young couple who can bring it back to life. It was once the most enchanting house on the entire street. If you could have only seen it when the Remington's lived here. Not a blade of grass out of place! Not a crack in the paint nor loose picket on the fence. This house radiated the love that its owners had for each other. Such a tragedy what happened----such a tragedy." Tom looked down at the sidewalk and gently shook his head from side to side. You could see the sadness ---you could *feel* the sadness in his voice. Tom seemed to be frozen in time for a few seconds before snapping his attention back to his clients.

At first Diane didn't want to ask what had happened. It just didn't feel right at that moment. But, there was a distinct pause in the conversation. "What happened?" Diane inquired gently. She was too curious not to ask. Then there was a long pause.

Tom raised his head and looked toward the mountains---his eyebrows furrowed and his eyes squinted from the sun. One could tell that no matter how many times he had told the story, it was still painful for him.

"Brandon and Marilyn were more in love than you can even imagine. Both were retired and were enjoying their 'golden' years. You would see them puttering around in the yard everyday---as long as the weather permitted. In the winter, they would bundle up and take freshly baked cookies to

17

their neighbors before settling down in front of their own fireplace to read or to talk. Well—long story short—Brandon loved to fly and pilot his own, small plane whenever he had a chance. I think they were going on a short trip to visit relatives when the plane crashed into the side of that mountain over there. (There was more to the story but Tom was not going to go into it.) Such a tragedy. Didn't have children---I guess that was a good thing---but other family members were devastated, of course. Town's folk mourned the couple for years after the accident. Brandon's sister, Bonnie, couldn't even stand the thought of anyone else taking over this house. She even left it totally intact---furniture, clothes, everything—till the windows started getting broken out. She finally gave everything away and boarded up the windows. It's been this way for at least the past fifteen years. Finally, some relatives convinced her to sell it---so here I am. Like I said---I'm here to show you this *fine* abode."

As Tom fumbled with the heavy ring of keys to find the right one, Diane could feel the excitement building in her chest. She couldn't wait for Tom to open the front door!

Tom stopped before turning the key completely then said, "Now folks, remember this house hasn't seen a dust mop nor a broom in many a year. We've got a cleaning crew scheduled to work on it but they can't get here until Saturday. Ya just gotta look past the years of sitting."

"Well, here we go!" John said rather reluctantly as he surveyed the front door. He had seen the outside and feared the inside couldn't be much better. He saw the excited look on Diane's face but just couldn't seem to muster any excitement on his part. "Give it a look," he calmly said to himself. "Try not to hurt yourself in doing so, either."

The front door creaked open on hinges that hadn't seen a drop of oil in at least fifteen years. Creak....creeeeak...That didn't bother Diane. To her the creaking noise was the house's own voice, beckoning her to come in.

"Oh my! Look at this!" Diane instantly exclaimed as she looked into the living room. She could envision the main room with its beautiful fireplace and warming hearth. A nice painting or antique mirror would hang above it and reflect the lighting and warmth of the room. Exquisite-hardwood floors would offer a deep, walnut color and an accent rug would be between the sitting area and the fireplace. Diane's eyes glimmered as the room unfolded before her.

"Obviously, I'm not seeing what you're seeing," John cautiously commented. To him, this house was one big mess. He was a handyman and could fix almost anything, but this might be the biggest challenge of his life. He just didn't know if he wanted to bite off this big of a project. He even wondered if they had enough money to manage the repairs that would be needed. As he glanced around, he couldn't even see one square foot that didn't need something!

Diane's eyes were lit up as large as any could possibly be. She grinned from ear to ear. "This is even better than I could have imagined!"

John looked around---puzzled ---searching for what Diane was talking about. He saw old, faded carpet, partially pulled back from one corner, exposing the dull, wood flooring underneath. The wallpaper was faded and terribly outdated and the chandelier was coated with a thick layer of dust. It probably didn't even work any longer. A large, fireplace mantle was the focal point of the living room but the paint was dull and cracking. "You can't find a mantle like that anymore---hand-carved you know. Pretty special for a home of this size. And the hardwood floors are a plus, too. Fix 'um up and their good forever," Tom interjected in his agent persona. A layer of dust rested on every surface, covering up what faded color remained. Basically, it was a mess—a terrible mess.

Diane walked over to the corner of the room and tugged on a piece of carpet that had already been pulled back from the corner. A small poof of dust swirled around her shoes, covering them with a fine layer of powder. She sneezed but didn't seem to mind.

"John, these hardwood floors will look absolutely beautiful once they're refinished. You know---remember when you refinished the Adkins's old hardwood floors? They said they looked better than new!" Then Diane looked down at the floor with a puzzled look on her face. "Look! It's interesting that the scuff marks are like this. It looks like the people who lived here had a little dance floor all of their own right here in front of the fireplace. See? The scuff marks go around the edge of the room just like someone was dancing around and around. Hmmm."

Thinking nothing more of it, Diane anxiously walked toward the kitchen. Although the windows were boarded and kept out most of the light, thin rays of sunshine pushed through the cracks to show that if Diane bought this house, she would have a sunny kitchen every morning. She always dreamed of having a bright, cheerful kitchen where she could sip on her coffee and contemplate her duties for the day.

"Perfect," she thought. "There's nothing better than sippin' that morning cup of coffee and watching the sun come up across the yard." The little, one-bedroom efficiency they were currently living in only had one window. It faced north and any morning sun was blocked by the large shrub that had grown next to the house on the east side.

"I will have to say," John responded, "If we had as much money to fix up the house as it's gonna cost to buy the house, we could really make it into a showplace. Not that I actually see it like you do, but I'm goin' on pure, blind faith. Faith in you, my darlin' and love of my life." John winked at Diane as he finished talking. He knew in his heart that if she wanted this house, even in the condition it was in, he would make sure they got it. He would worry about what to actually do with it later.

The kitchen was laid out perfectly as far as Diane was concerned. There was ample cabinet space and a few of the upper cabinet doors had glass inserts. Diane had always liked the idea of displaying her beautiful, floral china. It didn't get used that often---she saved it for special, family dinners—so the thought of at least displaying it to be admired on a daily basis made her smile. She loved flowers. She loved pretty things but what girl didn't?

A curved, window seat was nestled under the large, bay window at one end of the kitchen. Diane's mind whirled as she looked at the window seat---- she would choose just the right fabric to coordinate with the new wallpaper she would pick out and would make both a window-seat cushion and window treatments out of the same fabric. She was talented at sewing and could make professional-looking window treatments in no time at all. OK— she had that figured out. How lovely it was going to be!

While Diane was dreamily decorating the kitchen as any woman would do, John noticed that the linoleum flooring would have to be replaced. John knew that he could get most of the building supplies through his uncle's lumberyard and would also get a discount. The labor would be entirely up to him. Of course, Diane would help as much as she could. He could show her what to do. She was not afraid of hard work. She was also very good with painting and trim work. No one could paint around windowpanes quite as good as Diane. When she painted, there was never a drop of paint on the glass.

*"It'll take at least a day just to tear the flooring up."* John mumbled to himself.

"Well, this cottage certainly has a lot of character!" Tom exclaimed lest he appear too quiet. He wanted to give the young couple all the time they needed to really study the house, but he was already pretty sure Diane was putting up the "SOLD" sign in her mind. He wasn't that confident about John's decision but in his many years in the real estate business, he came to realize that the woman has to be happy. A husband might convince his wife not to take a house for various reasons, but if the wife really, really wants it, it is probably going to happen---a lot of work or not.

The master bedroom was the next area of interest. As John and Diane entered the door, both were taken back by the size. A small cottage would normally not have a master bedroom that included space for a small, sitting area in front of a second fireplace. Even John could see the value in this sort of arrangement. The house was small, yet it had many of the amenities that are found in larger homes---a fireplace in the living room?----a window seat in the kitchen?---a fireplace in the master bedroom? It just seemed too good to be true!

Diane could see herself here, years in the future, after the children are safely tucked in their beds. John and Diane could settle in, in front of the warmth of the fireplace, sipping on a glass of wine. In comfy pajamas, they would discuss the events of the day, make decisions that needed to be made, or just hold each other while watching the flickering embers slowly dying to a warm glow.

"There was a lot of love in this home, John," Diane said seriously. "I can feel it. I can't explain it. I just feel it." As she spoke, Diane's eyes drifted around the ceiling; it was as if she were searching for the spirits of those who once occupied the home.

John gave a quick glance to Tom who acknowledged his glance with a nod. They didn't say a word. In a second, Diane was heading down the hall. Tom and John followed. At the end of the hall were two bedrooms that would be playfully decorated for Carla and Randell. Mind you, Carla and Randell had not even been born yet, but somehow Diane knew she would have a boy and a girl and she had the names picked out from the time she was fifteen years old. Luckily, John agreed with her choice of names.

The bedrooms were small but had large windows that overlooked the backyard. The rooms were bright and cheerful, or at least, they would be after Diane got hold of them.

"Perfect!" Diane said again. She twirled around to face the men with a large smile on her face. "Perfect!"

"Is it a deal?" Tom asked somehow believing that if the sale price were right, it really was going to be a deal.

"Why don't we study the price, consider what renovations must be done immediately, and then make an offer tomorrow?" John said, realizing that as the man of the family, he needed to veer away from the emotional and stick to the practical side of buying the house.

"That sounds like a great idea!" Tom said. "I'll talk to you tomorrow after you've both had time to figure everything out. We'll take a proposal to the owner if you want and go from there." Tom smiled from ear to ear. He sensed that this young couple would be perfect for the house and he also sensed that the owners would like them to have it.

John and Diane thanked Tom for taking the time with them and promised to call him the following day. That night, they discussed the sale price of the house and estimated what it would take in time and money to make the house livable. Of course, they would be doing most of the work themselves. "Labor of love." Diane would say. "Anytime you put your blood, sweat, and tears into a home, it becomes a part of your being---a part of your essence of life."

"Ya know, John?" she said inquisitively. "I can't explain it but I already feel a special connection to this house. It's almost like we were supposed to come here, buy this house, and put it back into its original condition. I think we were meant to do this."

"Well, I'm willing to take it on if you are!" John said with conviction. Diane threw her arms around John and kissed him affectionately. They went to bed that night excited about their decision. Diane, too nervous to sleep, let her mind whirl with thoughts of glass-front cabinets, hardwood floors, and cobblestone walkways. She finally tired and fell into a deep sleep. John fell asleep right away--- the mere thought of all the work made him so exhausted that sleep came quite easily for him.

Early the next morning, John called Tom at the real estate office, made a verbal offer, and then ran by to sign the contract. Tom contacted the owners who hesitantly accepted the offer. "Oh, I know this is the right thing to do," said the daughter of the owner. "It is just that one of the only things left of our Aunt Marilyn and Uncle Brandon is that old house. Mom talked about it all the time before she passed away. Well, we need to move on, I reckon. We will sign the papers so the young couple can begin their lives. I think this is just what the house needs." With that, the process of changing ownership was put into motion.

"Congratulations!" Tom cheerfully said as he heard John answer on the other end of the line. "Your offer has been accepted-----you are now the proud owners of that fine abode!" It was humorous to use that term. It always produced a laugh.

John didn't know if he should be glad or not, but he knew how much Diane wanted the house so he was determined to give it his best. Diane had a way of always knowing the right thing to do so John had to respect her decision. Diane screamed out of excitement when John told her about the phone call.

She ran over to him, threw her arms around him in a huge, bear hug, and almost knocked him to the ground.

"You'll see!"  Diane screamed.  "You'll be so proud of what we do to this house and how it'll become who we really are!  I just can't wait! Let's go tell our parents!"

3

They took ownership of the house in early March when the mornings and evenings were still really cool and fear of frost still hung in the air. A few, tiny perennials were starting to peak their heads through the earth along the back fence although most of the rose bushes had been long dead.  They worked night and day getting the little house presentable enough just to move into.  They could do all of the renovations once they move in, but first it had to be clean and workable. They took care of all of that while they remained living in the little efficiency.  Then it was finally time to move their belongings and stock the kitchen.

Before John returned home one day, a strange thing happened. Diane was scurrying around the yard when she noticed an elderly lady walking along the side of the house. Diane had never seen her before, but she really didn't know any of her neighbors yet. When Diane ran out to introduce herself, she couldn't find the lady.  She thought it was rather strange but she didn't have too much time to think about it.  After all, there was still so much work to do.  Diane felt for sure she'd see her again sometime. Diane never thought a thing about it and didn't even mention it to John at the time.

Much work had to be done on the house so they jumped in right away. Carpet was removed, wood floors were refinished, and fresh paint was applied everywhere. Once the main repairs and updates were made, John and Diane tackled the yards. The backyard had once been a floral haven for the owners. Although the trees and shrubs had become terribly overgrown and totally unruly, one could see remnants of rose bushes along the back fence. Diane found something quite interesting as she surveyed the yard to imagine the new landscape design. She couldn't help but notice one particular pink rosebush that appeared to be in excellent condition. Obviously, it had been cared for when nothing around it had. Diane remembered from her garden magazines how roses need constant and careful attention to maintain their beauty. Where the other rose bushes were overgrown, untrimmed, and mostly dead, this one bush had obviously been trimmed recently and showed new, vibrant growth. Pink buds covered the branches, waiting to burst into full color. Whatever her new landscape design entailed, it would definitely include that rose bush.

Diane felt it was really strange that someone would take care of this isolated rosebush and give no care to anything else in the yard. Perhaps, she thought, it was the same lady that she had seen earlier in her yard. Maybe she has been reaping the fruits of her labor and has been enjoying the roses for herself since the home had been abandoned. In any case, Diane was happy to allow the lady to continue getting roses from the bush she cared for and would tell her that next time she saw her---if she ever did.

The kitchen turned out to be one of the best places in the house. The torn linoleum on the floor was replaced with white, ceramic tile and a fresh coat of white paint made the kitchen cabinets appear almost new. Diane sewed a pink floral seat cushion and the window treatment above the windows. With the morning sun pouring in from the east, Diane knew it was going to be a cozy retreat--just perfect for that early morning cup of coffee.

Diane was most pleased with the glass inserts in the kitchen cabinets. When she saw the house for the first time, she knew that they would be the perfect place to store her lovely floral china. Carefully resting each plate in the little groove at the back of the shelf, she made a beautiful display that certainly added to the décor of the room. Now, every day, she could enjoy looking at her china, quite a change from it being hidden in boxes in the hallway closet of their tiny efficiency. Glancing around the room, Diane was very pleased at how pretty and sunny the kitchen had become. She knew it must have looked that way many years ago when the previous owners had it. She often wondered what they were like and if they loved the house as much as she loved it already.

The living room was also quite special. Once the old, faded carpet was removed and the hardwood floors were refinished, the living room took on a whole-new personality. John removed the paint from the fireplace and refinished it to the natural-wood finish. The fireplace had been beautiful before but now it could be termed "majestic." The intricately carved details came alive with the new finish. With new wallpaper and fresh paint on the moldings, the room was ready to welcome the furnishings to make it a real living room. John and Diane didn't have all of the pieces of furniture that they wanted but they could continue to add as their budget would allow.

"You know what is so interesting about our living room, John?" Diane asked as they were enjoying dessert after dinner one evening.

"Besides the fact that we don't have a rug to go under the coffee table and I know you will want to find one for there?" John replied trying to second guess what she was about to say. From John's experience, Diane wanted to put a rug under everything---under the kitchen table----under the coffee table--under the entry table--even under the small table on the porch!

"No! I am not talking about that! Yes, it is true that we need a rug in there to tie together all of the décor but I am talking about something that we saw when we first pulled up the carpet."

"I know you mentioned that you noticed scuff marks but that is about all you said," John said casually.

"Remember, I said that it looked like the room had been used for dancing. The scuff marks or worn marks looked like they were made from someone dancing on the wood floor. I bet if we asked around, we would find out that the owners loved to dance! Wouldn't that be fun to find out!" Diane sometimes got excited about the simplest things.

"Well, we have plenty of time to do all kinds of things. Since the weather is getting warmer, everyone will be out walking in the neighborhood and I am sure we will be meeting many more of the people on our street."

"Yes, and I want to meet that lady whom I saw the other day on the side of the house. You know, I think she is also the one who is caring for the rosebush in the back by the fence. I wonder if she will still come around now that we have taken up residence here. She is certainly welcome! Actually, we can use all of the help we can get!" Diane knew the amount of work that would be needed to get the yard in order.

Sometimes Diane made up answers to the questions she had in her head. *Why did the little old lady care for just that single rosebush---if she, in fact, did?* Diane's answer was, *"Maybe she gave the former owners that bush and she had a special connection to it. Maybe it's an heirloom and she's trying to preserve its existence!"*

Chapter Two
Brandon's and Marilyn's Summer
May 1932

Brandon was a tall, handsome, young man almost twenty-six years old. His build was fairly muscular, showing the fruits of his hard work down at the gym. His dark, brown hair and even darker eyes made him very attractive to women of all ages. He had successfully completed four years at the university and was settled into his career as an accountant in his father's firm. He had always loved working with numbers and had a special way of getting balance sheets to figure accurately on the first try. Maybe it was because he grew up with a father who loved accounting, or maybe it was just a natural skill that he was born with. He didn't know, but he liked what he was doing for a living and felt thankful to have a successful business that he could immediately go into after graduation. Brandon was a serious businessman and soon the entire town dubbed him as the town's shining star. The townspeople watched as Brandon was selected to lead one town committee after the other. He really was a shining star and there was no limit as to what he would be able to accomplish in his lifetime.

Socially, he was considered one of the most eligible bachelors in the town. Besides being very handsome, Brandon had the personality to charm anyone. He had a great sense of humor and had a knack for telling jokes to people of all ages. Children loved him because he had a way of making them feel that they were especially important to him. The older townsfolk admired him for his accomplishments and the time he spent helping them with their projects. He was a buddy and a pal to most of the single men in the town, even those who were jealous of the attention he always received from the young ladies. He was definitely the most eligible and desirable bachelor.

After putting his whole life and almost every waking moment into building his career, Brandon decided that he wanted a wife at his side. He had dated most of the beautiful girls in the town but no one had really been the right one for him. Every relative had tried to pair him up with girls that they knew, some even from out of state, but again, nothing seemed to work out. Then one summer morning everything changed.

Marilyn's mother and father had relocated to Slaton just as she was finishing college. She was much too busy to help them with the move although she would have welcomed a break from her studies. Finally, the summer had come and it was her chance to visit her parents and see their new house.

Slaton was a small town boasting a population of only 2800. It was only about thirty minutes from a much larger city, so people living there felt they had the best of both worlds. They could live in a small, close-knit community and at the same time, have all the conveniences of a much larger city. Meanwhile, Marilyn's parents enjoyed the more relaxed, laid-back lifestyle of the little town they now call 'home'.

Marilyn was a tall, thin, young lady with flowing, blonde hair. Her eyes were a beautiful, aqua blue in color. Her father told her she had a little of the sky and a little of the ocean in her eyes. She studied music at the North Texas State College and had only one more year to completion. Since the time that she was a tiny girl, Marilyn loved to sing and dance and enjoyed it more than anything else she had ever done. As a four-year-old, her mother enrolled her in the Catherine Sue School of Dance down at the corner of Main Street and Frankfort in her hometown of Brennan. As the dance recitals came around, Marilyn's mother got with the other mothers to sew the elaborate dance costumes. Marilyn loved getting dressed up in the costumes but her real love was when she "lost" herself in the dance routine. It was as if she were in another world. She flowed with the music and appeared to glide across the stage. Everyone said she had natural talent. She was certainly better than most of the girls whose parents signed them up for dance to improve coordination. Marilyn had the look of a dancer. She was pencil thin, had perfect coordination, and had natural dance ability. Along with ballet lessons came tap and jazz. Marilyn was equally as good in those dance classes, too. Marilyn danced at her lessons, she danced down the sidewalk as she made her way back to her house, and she danced continually the rest of the day, moving from room to room, dancing while completing her homework or finishing her chores.

"Does that girl ever stop dancing?" her father asked her mother when he noticed her pirouetting across the living room floor.

"Isn't it nice that she enjoys dancing so much and is so good at it?" her mother replied as only a true, loving mother would.

"You'd just think she would get tired of all of that twirling and dipping and lunging and such. I certainly would!" said her father just as Marilyn went floating into the kitchen in another ballerina movement, arms rising up above her head while spinning on her toes.

Marilyn continued her lessons all the way through high school and even spent two summers in New York attending classes at the New York School of Ballet. It was quite a stretch for her parents to finance her lessons there but, they felt it was important since it appeared that she was going to eventually make her career out of singing and dancing.

In college, Marilyn was the main attraction in all of the musicals and play performances. The professors wrote in dance scenes whenever they could just to highlight her dance ability. Although Marilyn had grown up and no longer pirouetted through the living room, it was obvious by the way she looked and the way she stood that ballet was in her blood. More than one person noticed how she sometimes stood erect with heels together and toes pointing out even when she didn't know she was doing it.

Marilyn only had one more semester at the university and she would be out in the real world. She had been toying with the idea of getting a job with the dance company in Lubbock-- the large town only a few miles away from where her parents had moved. She liked the idea of doing what she had prepared herself to do and at the same time be close to her parents in a smaller town environment. She was excited at the thought of spending the summer with her parents in Slaton, in an environment away from the university town where she attended school.

"I am so excited you are spending the summer with us! I can't wait for you to see the new house that we have picked out. Of course, you might want to redo your room, but I think you will find it to be very comfortable. We can go to the store and pick out new bedding to coordinate with the curtains if you like, and maybe there is a rug that we would want to get. We will fix the room up just right for you!"

Marilyn's mother was so anxious for her to see their new home. She also looked forward to having her only daughter there for breakfast each morning and for the special walks through the neighborhood. They used to do those things together before Marilyn went off to college.

"I am excited, too, Mom! Don't go to any trouble. I just want to relax after a stressful school year. Anything we do will be a nice change,"

Marilyn replied feeling the excitement.

In just a few days, Marilyn finished her semester at school and was ready to make the trip to her parent's home. It really wasn't too much of a drive---four hours at the most---but it would also give her time to think about what she would be doing with her life once she had graduated. Her mind seemed to twirl. So many things to think about! So many plans to make!

2

On the first morning after arriving at her parents' home, Marilyn decided to run down to the corner pharmacy to pick up a few items that she needed for her stay. She threw on a pretty floral sundress, her new sandals, and headed out the door. The Eblen Pharmacy was only three blocks from her parents' home.

'I'll be right back, Mom. Do you need me to pick up anything at the store?" she asked as she was reaching for her purse.

"No. Not a thing," her mother responded. "Don't forget that Aunt Linda wants us to meet her for lunch today. It's been so long since she's seen you. It should be a lot of fun." Marilyn smiled and nodded that she remembered. She always enjoyed seeing her Aunt Linda and actually looked forward to it today.

With that, Marilyn headed out the door, walked the short distance to the corner pharmacy and began searching for the items she needed. Picking up a few things, she walked back to the door to get a small basket for her purchases. Just like in all stores, she usually bought more items than she originally intended to buy and more than once she had to go to the front of the store to retrieve a basket or cart. Just as she reached the front of the store, she noticed a very handsome gentleman talking to someone on the sidewalk. Marilyn was taken back by the striking appearance this man made. She had to admit to herself that her heart did a little dance of its own at that moment. *Don't stare!* she told herself.

Turning around, and heading back to the aisles to shop, she heard the pharmacy door open. She couldn't help but glance around to see if the handsome gentleman was the one entering the door. Yes! He, too, needed to be in the pharmacy for something. How lucky! Marilyn immediately smoothed her hair --it had become blown during her walk. Rubbing her lips together insured her that she still had a layer of lipstick on her lips so that she wouldn't look so pale. *I can't believe I am acting this way,* she thought to herself, *I don't even know this man! He is married for all I know. What am I doing?*

As luck would have it, Brandon didn't even notice her. He didn't notice her hair that she straightened---he didn't notice the lipstick she had on her lips. He didn't even notice HER. He quickly grabbed a couple of items and zoomed out the door. He certainly seemed like a man on a mission and a man in a hurry to go somewhere----anywhere ELSE.

Marilyn made a mental note to try to find out more about whom this man was. With a sigh, she paid for her items and left the store. When she arrived home, her mother was in the kitchen putting together a casserole for dinner. Marilyn joined in and helped cut up onions and shred cheese. She thought about asking her mother if she knew of a man who might fit the description of the one at the pharmacy but changed her mind. That could be done later, she thought.

Lunch was fun. Marilyn and her mother met Aunt Linda at the ladies' tearoom. Maudie's had been a mainstay in town for almost thirty years. The young mother who originally started the tearoom was now a grandmother but the quality of the menu only got better and better over time.

Aunt Linda was six years older than Marilyn's mother. There were three children in their family--- Randell, the firstborn; Linda, the middle child; and Brenda, the baby of the family. Randell became a dentist and had an office in a neighboring town. Aunt Linda was a schoolteacher for many years, and eventually became principal of the junior high school in town. She had recently retired but continued to tutor students from time to time. Brenda, Marilyn's mother, was a homemaker but very actively involved in the community and the school system. She volunteered hundreds of hours each year for fundraising.

Marilyn, her mother, and her aunt sat in the sunny side of the tearoom, next to the front sidewalk.

Most people wanted to sit in that location where they could casually glance at the people walking down the walk. People-watching is a practiced sport in Slaton.

"Oh look! There's Janie Lou. Remember her? Boy! She's really gained weight since I've seen last." said the lady at the next table over.

"Look at Mary's precious little girl! Spitt'n image of her mom, isn't she?" another people watcher exclaimed at the table near the door. Just listening to the lunch crowd could be quite entertaining.

Just when the ladies were being served their salad plates, Marilyn glanced out the window very casually. *Oh, my gosh!* Marilyn said to herself. *There's that handsome gentleman I saw just this morning at the pharmacy!* Marilyn tried not to let the excitement she felt show. She certainly didn't want her mother and aunt to notice how rapidly her heart was beating. She didn't want to stare out the window---they would surely see who she was staring at so she casually glanced away from the window as nonchalantly as possible.

"Oh, Marilyn! Look! Brandon is standing right out there on the sidewalk! You don't know Brandon but he's the most wonderful, young gentleman I've ever known! I'm dying to introduce you to him!" Aunt Linda exclaimed barely able to contain her excitement at an allowable level. "Really! He's considered the most eligible bachelor in this town. He's successful, handsome as you can see, and everyone absolutely loves him. I think he's only five or six years older than you. That's perfect."

Marilyn could barely contain her excitement. *"Oh, my gosh! Can anyone see how hard my heart is pounding?"* she wondered not saying a word.

"You're still the matchmaker, aren't you, Linda!" Marilyn's mother commented already knowing the answer. "He does look like a fine, young man but you and I both know there is no one who's really going to be good enough for our baby here."

"Oh, Mother, surely I can find someone who would treat me as well as Dad has treated you all of these years. I'm sure your mother and father didn't think he was good enough for you either," Marilyn said with a grin as she sipped her peach tea.

Marilyn barely got the words out of her mouth when Aunt Linda sprang up from her chair and headed for the door. "Excuse me! I'll be right back!" She was on a mission to capture Brandon before he had a chance to get away.

Marilyn was excited but a little embarrassed at the same time. It was quite different meeting a man who was snagged off the front sidewalk by your aunt versus being introduced in a college class or casually meeting someone at the student union center at school. She really didn't know how she should react.

"Oh look!" her mother said. "She's bringing him in the tearoom!"

*Holy moly! I wonder what he's going to think about this!* Marilyn thought to herself as she conceded to the fact that Aunt Linda was going to introduce the two. She just hoped it wouldn't totally frighten him away where she would never get to know him under "normal" circumstances.

"Darling," Aunt Linda said as she walked up to the table holding Brandon's hand. Aunt Linda had a way of talking as she tilted her head to one side smiling. "This is that wonderful, young man I was telling you about earlier. This is Brandon Remington."

"It's such a pleasure meeting you, Brandon," Marilyn said as sweetly as she could. "I really hope my wonderful aunt did not coerce you into coming in." Marilyn laughed timidly. She could feel her heart fluttering. Marilyn thought Brandon was handsome when she first saw him outside of the pharmacy, but at three feet away, he was *strikingly* handsome!

"Oh, certainly not! I've had the wonderful pleasure of seeing your aunt on several occasions and must say she's one of the loveliest ladies in the entire town. I've equally had the opportunity to meet your beautiful mother since her arrival here and, therefore, would not be able to pass up the opportunity to meet the daughter and niece of such fine ladies," Brandon shook Marilyn's and then her mother's hand. Marilyn felt tingly all over. She couldn't believe it----*just couldn't believe it!*

Just as his comments ended, the young waitress arrived at their table to refill their tea classes.

"Don't let me interrupt your lunch. I have to get back to the office anyway. Ladies---enjoy your lunch," Brandon said with a big smile on his face as he turned and left the tearoom.

The ladies sipped at their peach tea and had conversation but Marilyn didn't remember much of what was said. She was mesmerized and in somewhat of a daze. She tried hard to enter in on the conversation but her real thoughts were on Brandon. *What a wonderful guy,* she thought to herself. *And so handsome, too!*

Brandon had been introduced to a hundred girls, in almost the same fashion that Aunt Linda introduced him to Marilyn. He would always smile and say just the right things. He knew how to be charming; in fact, it came to him naturally. Usually he didn't follow-up with anyone but he felt something a little different this time. When he looked into Marilyn's eyes, he didn't see the usual, beautiful, young girl. This time, he couldn't really explain it, but something was different. He thought about it several times that day. *"What is it?"* he asked himself. *"I don't even know who she really is! Maybe I should get to know her better, then, ol' boy."* With that thought, he finished the work at his office and headed for home. But he thought about Marilyn----all the way home.

Dinner that night was delightful. Marilyn and her parents sat at the round, kitchen table that had been in the family for almost 50 years and discussed plans for her last year of college. They marveled at how quickly Marilyn had grown up. Her mother recalled taking her to her elementary school and waiting for her at the day's end. Now, at almost 20 years old, Marilyn had one more year before beginning a career of her own. Of course, she would certainly be welcome to stay with her parents as long as she needed to---to get on her feet. In fact, they would like that very much.

The casserole that Marilyn and her mother had prepared earlier in the day was perfect with the compliment of salad and dessert. As Marilyn cleared the table, her mother commented to her father as Marilyn listened in, "Marilyn met Brandon Remington today. We were at Maudie's with Aunt Linda when she spotted Brandon outside on the sidewalk talking to one of his friends. Of course, Linda runs out the door, snags Brandon by the arm and brings him to our table so he can meet Marilyn."

"I bet that was a sight to see. Too bad I wasn't there," Mr. Davis said with a laugh.

"Oh, Dad, it really wasn't that bad," Marilyn said with a slight giggle, "He does seem to be a really nice guy from what I can tell."

Those words had barely gotten out of Marilyn's mouth when a faint knock was heard at the front door. Mrs. Davis pulled off her apron that she had forgotten to take off before sitting down at the table and headed for the front door. She could only see the top of someone's head through the fan-shaped window at the top of the door. She opened the door.

"Why Brandon! How nice to see you again!" Mrs. Davis said loudly enough so that both Marilyn and her father could hear in the kitchen. "Won't you please come in?"

"Oh, no, Mrs. Davis. I don't want to interrupt your dinner or anything." Brandon said as he smelled the aroma of the casserole that was still in the air. "I just thought that if Marilyn was here and didn't have anything to do this evening, we might go for a walk around the neighborhood. I would love to show her the small park by the creek and some of the other areas that she might not even know about yet."

Mrs. Davis knew that Marilyn did not have anything scheduled for the evening and would probably love to go on a walk. In fact, what girl would NOT want to go for a walk with Brandon? Even though Mr. and Mrs. Davis had only been members of the community for a short time, they had heard of what a good reputation Brandon had made for himself. It would be great for Marilyn to have a good friend to do things with while she was here for the summer.

"That sounds like a delightful thing to do this evening. Please come in, Brandon, and I will go ask Marilyn." Mrs. Davis motioned for Brandon to sit in the living room while she turned toward the kitchen. Marilyn was already entering the living room.

"Hi, Brandon! How are you this evening?" Marilyn didn't want to sound too excited. Inside, however, she was dancing---and skipping---and twirling!

"Marilyn, I thought that maybe, with your mother's permission, of course, you would be interested in going for a little walk around the neighborhood. There is a little park down by the creek and it is really beautiful this time of the year. In fact, I have heard that there is a giant goldfish in the creek. I think they call it a 'koi.' Rumor has it that it is about eighteen inches long and is solid orange. I would like to see if we could see it. What do you think?" Brandon said with a special glimmer in his eye.

"Oh, I would love to do that! Mom, do you need me for anything tonight? Do you need me to help you with the dishes?" Marilyn asked politely. She already knew when the answer was going to be.

"Hun, your father knows how to dry dishes. He can certainly stand in for one night. You go ahead and have fun." Mrs. Davis was almost as excited as she knew Marilyn was. "I hope you find that fish you're looking for." With that, Marilyn and Brandon headed out the door.

Brandon looked at Marilyn and couldn't believe she was actually walking next to him. He felt a special closeness that he had never felt before. He really wanted to put his arm around her but knew it was way too soon for that. He couldn't risk upsetting her in any way so he decided to just be very cordial and keep his arms to himself. Besides, he worried, if he put his arms around her, then he would want to hold her very tight, and then he wouldn't be able to control his urge to kiss her! *"No-no-no---not now---too soon---,"* he thought.

Brandon and Marilyn walked down the front sidewalk and then headed south toward the park near the creek. Brandon felt good having such a beautiful young lady by his side. He also wanted to know what the magic was about her and why he felt something different when their eyes first met. As they crossed the street, Brandon leaned down and picked a wildflower from the side by the street.

"You don't know we have flower shops just scattered around the town, do you?" he said as he handed her the small purple flower. It really was pretty small. "Yep! No one would believe it, but the flowers are actually FREE!" he said as if trying to convince her this was a true story. "If you need flowers to cheer you up, all you have to do is bend down and pick one from the free floral shops found on about every corner. Now, if you want a large bouquet, like for a birthday or wedding or something, you can go right down to Pauline's

Flower and Gift Shop. She'll fix you right up. Actually, Pauline retired some time ago, but her daughters, Jan and Barbara, will make you the most beautiful floral arrangements. Only thing is---you have to pay for those."

Marilyn couldn't help but laugh. The flimsy little wildflower that Brandon handed her had already started drooping and a couple of the petals had already fallen off.

"Oh, gee!" Marilyn exclaimed with fake enthusiasm. "I don't think I've ever seen a flower of such magnificence! *Surely*, even the kings of England never saw such marvelous feats of nature!" The poor flower continued to droop further.

"My name's not *Shirley*, but I will forgive you this one time." Brandon joked, hoping she got it. She did. Both of them burst into laughter.

Walking down the sidewalk to the park, Brandon turned to Marilyn from time to time and wondered how he could be so lucky. He felt comfortable with her from the very beginning. The conversation flowed easily and they seemed to enjoy each other's company very much.

"Oh look! Another flowershop! This time the daily pick is yellow. Aren't you lucky!" Brandon pulled the limp flower from her hand and threw it to the ground. "Here, a fresh one this time for your hair." With that, Brandon turned facing Marilyn and gently placed the flower stem through a curl in her hair. He didn't realize that, by doing so, his heart was going to start racing. He hoped she didn't notice. *Wow! This lady has an effect on me!* If he had his wish, he would have placed the flower in her hair and then he would have held her face between his warm hands to plant a loving kiss on her lips. *But no—no—not now---too soon---- don't blow it!*

"Just what I wanted!" Marilyn exclaimed. Their eyes met and that magic Brandon referred to earlier was again showing its head. Both seemed to freeze in their steps. Then just as quickly, each turned to continue the walk to the park. The seconds of silent were definitely noticed. Brandon felt the electricity and, in his heart, he knew she felt it, too.

Just a few more steps and they were walking on the cool, green grass of the park near the creek. The grass rolled gently over the slopes, plush with a deep-green color. Beautiful trees towered majestically, reaching to the clouds, branches reaching out over the creek. A soothing waterfall added to the comforting sounds of the birds' musical chirps. The creek widened at one point, making a peaceful and still pond before it poured over a rock dam at one end. From there, the water danced and skipped over the rocks and tree roots, curving its way around to another peaceful opening of water--- a larger, serene pool of water near the end. Amateur fishermen and children learned about their sport in this area of the creek. More than once, casting line was found hanging from the trees overhead. Everyone loved walking along the worn path, catching glimpses of darting fish and an occasional turtle or two. Tall trees hung down to the water's edge with large, fully exposed roots on the water's side. Kids loved climbing around on the roots and skipping flat stones across the water. The lush foliage overhead was an umbrella, blocking the summer sun and its harsh fingers. The park and creek had never looked more beautiful.

*"Is it really this beautiful here or is it because of Marilyn?"* Brandon thought to himself. He felt that he knew the answer already.

"Brandon?" Marilyn asked softly. "How long have you lived here?"

"Oh, I've been here all of my life, Marilyn. Well, except when I went off to college. I love living in a small, close-knit community. I experienced living in a larger city during my college years but was anxious to get back here. I guess I will be here the rest of my life." Brandon was serious in his answer. A small rabbit scurried across their path, stopped to rise up on its hind legs, and then looked at the couple before scurrying away.

"Let's walk down to the water to see if we can find that fish. I personally haven't seen it, but I have heard reports that it is a giant goldfish a foot and a half long." Brandon also felt that would give him more time to be with Marilyn.

They walked to the edge of the pond and looked in. The water was dark and filled with dark-green moss. There was no sign of the mysterious orange fish.  They really didn't care.  They just enjoyed being together. Besides, since they didn't see it this time, they would have to come back again.  What a wonderful excuse to relive this evening!

The sun had been slowly fading, making the sky more pink than gold. Brandon realized they would just have enough time to walk back to the Davis house before it got dark.

"We'd better head back, Marilyn.  I don't want your parents getting upset with me for getting you back too late," Brandon said with complete seriousness. Then he continued, "Now, don't think I haven't bought about kidnapping you tonight--but somehow I don't think I could get away with it." His eyes danced as he tried to act seriously for a minute. Marilyn laughed, playfully slapping his arm.

"I can't tell you how much I 've enjoyed being with you tonight, Brandon." Marilyn said softly.  "This is probably the prettiest park I've ever seen.  And ya know what?"

"What?" Brandon responded.

"I bet we'll see that fish someday.  We just have to have faith."

With that comment, Brandon reached around Marilyn's shoulder and gave her a slight hug. Brandon was a little hesitant at first, not really knowing what Marilyn would think about that.  He didn't want to seem too forward.  After all, this was the first time they had ever been together alone. He had resisted all afternoon, but he finally gave in. He finally negotiated with himself and agreed that a slight hug was permissible.

Reaching the front door of her home, Brandon said, "Marilyn, I don't know when I've enjoyed myself more. Do you mind if I call on you again sometime?"

"I'd love you to. Thanks for a very lovely evening." Marilyn felt like she was floating five inches off the ground. She couldn't explain the chemistry that occurred when she saw Brandon. After all, she had seen many handsome, young men on her college campus. But there was never that tingling feeling when she looked at them. Marilyn turned to walk through the door and Brandon turned to walk down the sidewalk. He turned and glanced back but Marilyn had already closed the door. Marilyn leaned against the closed door breathing a deep sigh. The house was quiet. Her parents were probably reading in their bedroom, winding down from the day.

"Mom?" Marilyn called out. "I'm home." Marilyn's mother always wanted to know when she returned home. That is all she wanted to say right now, but inside, she was thinking that it was the best day she had ever spent in her life---in her entire life.

"OK, dear, hope you had a good time.'

"I did," Marilyn called out. "I'll tell you about it in the morning." Marilyn just wanted to take a long, hot bath and try to relive each and every moment she just spent with Brandon.  If she never saw him again, she would at least have memories of this night and no one could ever take that away from her!  She laughed when she thought about the flowers.  She felt her hair with her left hand and, surprisingly, the flower was still there, right where Brandon placed it.  She pulled it out of her hair and lay it on the side of the tub.  She stared at the limp flower and smiled.

*"I'm going to keep this,"* Marilyn said to herself.  *"That's kind of silly, isn't it?  After all, I'm not thirteen anymore and I'm not trying to remember my eighth-grade dance."*  Marilyn talked to herself all the time----but never out loud.

Marilyn relaxed in the tub filled with lavender-scented, bubble-bath crystals. She closed her eyes and leaned her head against the back of the tub. Thoughts floated through her mind----the flowers, the grass, the trees, the creek, the bunny, the conversation------the hug.  Marilyn relived the hug over and over and over.  She hoped she would never forget.

Sleepiness was approaching.  Marilyn got out of the tub, dried off with a soft, fluffy, white towel and put on her favorite nightgown.  Glancing at the flower on the side of the tub, Marilyn picked it up and put it in a small book in her drawer.

*"I don't care."* She thought to herself. *"I'm keeping it."*

When Brandon got home, he went straight to his room. He was hoping his sister would not realize he walked in the door. His sister, Bonnie, had a way of quizzing him about everything he did. "Where'd ya go? Who were ya with? What did ya do?" she would ask anytime he went anywhere. She was probably just very caring and very interested in her big brother, but Brandon took it that she was very nosy.

Bonnie was twenty-two years old. She loved her big brother dearly. Although he was four years older, they were very close and always watched out for each other. Bonnie loved it when Brandon brought his friends home to visit, especially when he was in college and she was still in high school. When Bonnie found out Brandon was coming in for the weekend and was bringing a friend or two, Bonnie's friends would conveniently drop by to visit. Brandon accused Bonnie of planning the impromptu visits but she just told him she had friends who loved to drop in unexpectedly. In the end, it all turned out fine. Brandon and his friends did exactly what they wanted to do and the girls would catch a glimpse of them from time to time. Bonnie had grown up from those days but she still remained tuned in to everything Brandon did.

As Brandon tiptoed past Bonnie's room, she called out, "OK, I hear ya. How'd it go tonight? Vickie told me she saw YOU walking some blonde to the park.  Did ya really think you could do anything without my finding out?"

"Park?  Walking to the park?" Brandon asked quizzingly.  "It must've been someone else.  I think she must've seen someone else." Brandon actually thought he could get by with that comment.

Without even seeing Brandon, Bonnie said, "Are ya wearing a light-blue golf shirt and cream-colored slacks?"  She knew it was Brandon for sure.

"Nope!  See---not me!"  Brandon called back to her as he jerked off his light-blue golf shirt and started unbuckling his belt on his cream-colored slacks.  Bonnie jumped up from her bed and ran out to the hallway.  She caught him just as he ran through his bedroom door.

"Caught ya!  Do you think you can put anything over on me?" They both died laughing.

Still holding his blue shirt in his hand, Brandon said, "This shirt is blue?  No, it's not.  It's light brown.  Remember, I'm colorblind."  That comment brought a lot of laughter also.

He threw his shirt into the laundry basket.  "OK, nosy one.  I took Mrs. Davis's daughter to the park to show her the creek in hopes that we would see that mysterious, orange fish that people have been talking about."

"That's nice, Brandon," Bonnie answered back calmly.  "Do you think you are going to see her again?"

Trying to act nonchalant about the whole thing, Brandon said, "Oh, I might. I have a lot of work to do this week so maybe I will take her out sometime next week."

"Well, are you going to at least CALL her this week so she's not left HANGING?" Bonnie responded theatrically.

"Oh, I doubt that she is HANGING!" Brandon said with theatrical emphasis. "I think she and her mother are going to be working on a lot of projects this week, so she probably wouldn't even notice."

Turning to Brandon with a very serious look on her face, Bonnie said, "Just do me a favor. Call her tomorrow or the day after and tell her how much you enjoyed her company. That is, if you really did. And then make plans to see her again." Bonnie had a way of barking out orders without it seeming that way. She could tell from the way Brandon acted that this Marilyn girl was, indeed, someone quite special.

"Guess I will do that just because you want me to. You know how much I love my baby sister!" Brandon said with a wide grin but rather sarcastically.

6

"Good morning," Marilyn said as she entered the kitchen. Her father was sitting at the kitchen table reading the morning paper. His glasses always slid down on his nose which gave him the option of looking over them when not reading. He glanced at Marilyn and noticed an extra bounce in her step. Her mother was cooking breakfast. In fact, it was the smell of bacon cooking that woke Marilyn from her sleep.

"There's just nothing as good as the smell of bacon frying." Marilyn said interrupted by a slight yawn. "You certainly can't smell bacon in the dorm and if you do choose it in the cafeteria, it isn't nice and crispy like the way you make it, Mom. It's kind of soft and greasy--kind of limp."

"I really like it crispy," her mother said. Marilyn knew her parents were anxious to hear about her evening walk so she decided to save them from waiting.

"I had a great time with Brandon last night. He can be really funny. He had me laughing most of the way to the park. Do you know about the park down by the creek? I hope you haven't been missing out on that!" Marilyn said excitedly.

"Oh, yes!" her mother said. "That is one of the first places we visited when we moved here."

"Have you heard that there is a large goldfish in that pond?" Marilyn asked sincerely.

"Ya know----I just don't know," her mother replied. "It would certainly be something if there were one."

Marilyn's father looked up from his paper and over his reading glasses. "Well, I'm glad you had a nice time, Dear. I'm sure Brandon did, too."

The family sat down to a breakfast of bacon, eggs, toast, and fruit. Orange juice was Marilyn's drink of choice while her parents had their usual cups of coffee.

"What are the ladies of the house planning for today?" asked Marilyn's father.

"Oh, we will probably run down to the fabric store and see about some new curtains for Marilyn's room. Do you have any errands you need for us to do for you?" Mrs. Davis asked.

"No, not really. You have fun. I should be home around 6:00 tonight." Mr. Davis said as he headed out the door.

Marilyn and her mother cleaned up the breakfast dishes and then got ready to go to the fabric store. Marilyn loved doing things with her mother. It was such a nice change from school and dorm life.

The day went by, but not without Brandon thinking about Marilyn several times. He knew she was out with her mother, shopping for fabric to make new curtains for her bedroom. He also knew that was their first full day together so they would be quite busy. There would be no way to get in touch with Marilyn so he made a mental note to call her the following day. He didn't know what was on her agenda but he knew he wanted to talk to her.

Brandon got up early the following morning, got ready for work, and headed to the office. Bonnie got up, not as early, but also prepared to go to the clinic where she worked as a physical therapist. She wondered if he would remember her orders at the same time that Brandon wondered what the best time of the day to call would be. Whatever, they were both on the right track.

Around 10:45 am, Brandon took a break in the work that he was doing and picked up the phone to call Marilyn. When his secretary entered his office to ask him a question, he promptly placed the phone down without saying a word. After answering her questions, Brandon again picked up the phone, asked his secretary to hold all calls, and dialed the number to the Davis home. It rang five times before someone picked up the phone. It seemed like it was forever. *"What if no one answers? What if they are out shopping again? I should have tried to call yesterday!"* Brandon's mind spun as he waited for each ring.

"Hello," Mrs. Davis answered in her most polite voice.

"Mrs. Davis, this is Brandon Remington." Brandon said as kindly as he could. "Is Marilyn there by any chance? I would like to talk to her for just a minute."

"Oh, Brandon, you just missed her. Her father wanted to take her to meet some people down at his law office. They should be back shortly after lunch, I would imagine. Should I tell her you called?" Even Mrs. Davis was disappointed that Marilyn was not there to receive the call.

"Yes, please. I just wanted to see if she would be interested in going to the ballet this weekend. I hear it is a stunning performance." Brandon said cheerfully trying to conceal his disappointment of Marilyn not being there. The part that bothered him was Marilyn's going to meet some people at her father's law firm. *Does that mean meeting his older friends, or does that mean that he has some young lawyer type or maybe more than one to introduce to his daughter?"* Brandon pondered to himself. He even thought to himself how silly it was for him to be thinking this way. He had never felt possessive about any other girl--- much less one he had never taken on an official date. *"I must be losing it!"* he thought.

"I don't know if Marilyn has anything planned for this weekend but I can tell you that ballet is one of her favorite arts. She is a dancer, you know, and when she was just a child, she danced throughout the house, from one end to the other. Why don't you call here this afternoon and ask her?" Mrs. Davis said wanting to go ahead and book the event for her daughter.

Brandon agreed to call Marilyn later in the afternoon but that didn't make him feel any better. He couldn't get her out of his mind. He also worried, imagining that she was having a wonderful lunch with some tall, dark, and handsome young attorney from her father's firm. He had never really thought about competition before. I guess he had never really cared this much before.

When Marilyn and her father arrived back home around 1:30 pm, her mother was waiting at the kitchen table, working on a new recipe box to hold her millions of recipes.

"Your friend called." Mrs. Davis said not even looking up from her task.

"Which friend?" Marilyn asked. "? She is supposed to call me sometime this week."

"No, Brandon called. He said something about going to the ballet this weekend."

Marilyn's heart started pounding rapidly. *"This is too good to be true,"* she thought. "Is he going to call back?" Marilyn tried not to sound too anxious, just interested. She didn't care if it were the ballet or a rodeo. Going anywhere with Brandon would be too good to be true!

"I think he'll call back sometime this afternoon. He's certainly a nice, young gentleman. Did you know that the ballet performance he wants to take you to is considered one of the finest in the country? I am anxious to see it myself."

Mr. Davis pulled up a chair and sat down at the table.

"We had a good time at the office this morning. I wanted Marilyn to meet my partner George, and to get to know the girls in the office. If she wants to do a little work in the office this summer, I can set that up for her," Mr. Davis said.

"Did she meet George's son, Mark?" Mrs. Davis inquired.

"Oh, yes. You didn't think George would let me bring Marilyn into the office without arranging for Mark to be there to meet her, did ya?"

"I figured something like that," she said.

What Marilyn didn't know was that George had wanted to set up a meeting between his son, Mark, and Marilyn for at least a year. Knowing how beautiful and smart Marilyn was, George was looking out for the best interest of his son. Mark was 28 and had been in a long-term relationship with a girl in the town that wasn't really working out. Although Mark really didn't say anything about wanting to meet anyone else, his parents knew he needed to move on in his life. Maybe Aunt Linda should get involved, Mrs. Davis thought to herself with a chuckle.

Mr. Davis helped himself to a tall glass of water as Marilyn poured a glass of lemonade for her mother and herself. She had just sat down at the table to join her mother when the telephone rang. Everyone knew it was Brandon calling back to ask Marilyn to the ballet. Marilyn rushed to answer.

8

"Hello?" Marilyn said into the receiver.

"Marilyn?" the man on the other end said. Marilyn didn't think it sounded like Brandon.

"This is Mark Bernett from the law office." Marilyn's heart sank. "I was wondering if you would be interested in driving into Greenville with me Friday night. There is a dinner party that I have been invited to and I think you would enjoy the people you would meet there. What do you think?"

Marilyn was caught totally off guard. She thought Mark was a really nice man but she was so enamored by Brandon. She really wanted to go to the ballet with Brandon more than anything else in the world but she didn't even know for what night the performance was scheduled or for what night he had tickets. Knowing that the performances were probably Friday AND Saturday really put her into a quandary. She also knew that her parents wanted her to date several men before she settled down

63

since she had had very little chance to date in college. What was she to do? Not really knowing what to do, she accepted the invitation. She couldn't tell him a lie, like she was already busy Friday night and then it turned out to be not true. Although she should have told him that she was supposed to go to the ballet but didn't know yet if the tickets were for Friday or Saturday, she just couldn't think that fast on her feet with Mark on the phone and her parents right there listening to the whole thing.

"That's great!" Mark exclaimed obviously pleased. "I'll pick you up Friday evening at 6:30pm. I look forward to seeing you again!"

Marilyn should have been excited about the prospect of going to a dinner party with a fine, successful gentleman. She should have been excited about meeting new friends and acquaintances. Before, she would have jumped at the chance, but now, everything was different. All she could think about was the phone call she was hoping to get from Brandon. Then she cringed at the thought of telling him she was already busy if he wanted to take her to the ballet on Friday. She didn't want to ruin anything with Brandon. Marilyn plopped down in the chair and let out a giant sigh. *Life can be so tough!* she thought.

"Mom! What should I have done? I didn't know what to do! I really want to go to the ballet with Brandon," Marilyn said almost tearfully, "But I got caught off guard! Oh! I think I really blew it!"

Before her mother could say a word, her father spoke up. "Marilyn, it is a good thing to meet many people and date others before you settle down. You are in the prime age for doing just that. I know you are pretty high on Brandon right now but a little competition never hurt anyone. Take it slowly, honey. You have your whole life to live. You'll see that it will all work out like it should in the end. Remember---everything works out the way it is supposed to."

Marilyn's father always had a way of calming everyone down in tense situations. He was wise and experienced--but he knew what she was going through inside. She was still his little girl.

"Sugar, it will be fine to go with Mark this Friday. Make it into a very positive experience. Meet as many new friends as you can. You'll have fun," her mother added.

Marilyn settled down a little bit. She was still nervous about Brandon calling. Within five minutes the phone rang again. The three of them looked at each other with eyes wide open. Marilyn ran to answer the phone.

9

"Hello?" she answered anxiously.

"Marilyn? Did your mother tell you I called this morning?" Brandon asked.

"Yes! She did. I'm sorry I wasn't here when

you called."

"Would you like to go to the ballet with me this Friday night?"

Marilyn's heart sank right into the floor. Not even knowing it, her body posture slumped. Her parents noticed. They both felt sorry for her but would not let it show.

"Oh, Brandon! Yes, yes! I would love to go to the ballet, but I can't go on Friday. I am busy Friday night! Oh, I am so sorry! The ballet is one of my favorite things. I love it!" Marilyn felt tears filling her eyes.

With that answer, Brandon's heart also sank. It was probably just as he had feared. Marilyn went to the office with her father and some tall, handsome man asked her out for Friday night. He knew it. He just knew it. But, thinking quickly, Brandon said, "How about Saturday night? I think I can exchange these tickets if you could go Saturday night."

In an instant, Marilyn's whole demeanor changed. A huge smile came on her face. She stood up straight. "Yes! I would love to go on Saturday. What time should I be ready?"

"Why don't I pick you up at 5:30? We'll have time to get a bite to eat and then drive to the performing arts building for the performance at 7:30. Will that work for you?"

"Yes. Certainly. I'll see you then." Marilyn

hung up the phone and then floated back to the table. On the way, she twirled around, did a deep bow, and then sat down grinning from ear to ear.

"See?" Her father said. "See how everything has a way of working out?" Actually, both her mother and father were quite relieved. They felt the anxiety that she was experiencing and wanted her to be happy. Marilyn had time to think about what she'd say to Brandon about her Friday night date. Maybe it wouldn't come up at all. She would figure that out later. For now, she just wanted to take a nap and fall asleep dreaming about Brandon.

The rest of the week went by slowly. Marilyn and her mother finished working on the curtains for her bedroom. Her father took her to the carpet store to pick out a new rug for under her bed, and then had the work done on her car that needed to be done. She was always thankful that her father looked after her car since she never thought about it. As long as it started, worked in reverse, and got her to where she was going, she didn't think about anything else. He checked on her oil changes, checked on her tires that she absolutely never looked at, and made sure the fluid levels were adequate for coolant and water.

Marilyn hoped that Brandon would call sometime before she saw him on Saturday, but then, she figured that was probably asking for too much. She would just be patient. She did spend a lot of time thinking about what she was going to wear and how she was going to fix her hair. She wanted to look perfect. She already knew that Brandon must have dated many, beautiful women so she wanted to look special.

"Mom, what do ya think I should wear Saturday night to the ballet?" Marilyn asked.

"Marilyn, why don't you wear that little black dress that you wore to the reception at the university? It is stunning on you. You look so sophisticated in black. Be sure to wear your new heels. How are you going to wear your hair? Should you go have it done at Judy's Beauty Shoppe?" her mother offered.

"That is exactly the dress I was thinking of wearing. But, instead of going to the beauty shop, I would rather do my hair myself. I think I will wear it up for a change."

"What do you think you'll wear Friday night?"

"Oh, I don't know yet. I'll figure that out by Friday." Marilyn answered casually.

Marilyn's mother could tell from her actions that she felt very differently about the two evenings. Marilyn was excited about Saturday night but was just accepting about Friday night. Interesting.

10

Marilyn had spent most of the day at the library researching material for an article that the university newspaper wanted her to write about dance companies. They wanted her to write it during the regular school year, but she was just too busy with all of her classes and then the extra practices and her volunteer work. She told them that she would gladly write it when she had time over the summer. Marilyn thought of a million things that she needed to do and she thought that she would have plenty of time over the summer. Probably there would not be enough time to do everything but she was going to try. As she glanced down at her watch, she realized that she only had about an hour to get home, get cleaned up, and get ready for Mark to pick her up. Furthermore, she never figured out what she was going to wear. She thought she would probably come up with something as she was taking her bath. Hopefully, what she decided on would be clean and neatly pressed.

Marilyn ran through the back door, into her bathroom, and immediately started her bath water. Her mother could hear her scurrying around and knew she did not have very much time to get ready. The bath was not the leisurely bath she remembered after the walk in the park. It was a quick in and out sort of thing with water dripping all over the floor since she was drying off and walking to her closet at the same time. Marilyn jerked a dress off the hanger, zipped it up and grabbed her shoes. She didn't feel like she looked 'striking' but that is about all she could muster in such a short time. She combed her hair into waves, straightened her bangs, and put tiny diamond studs in her ears. A light splash of makeup topped with compact powder and she only needed mascara and some lipstick. Whew! She got ready just in time for the knock at the door.

Marilyn heard her mother answer the door and greet Mark in her usual cheerful tone.

"You must be Mark," Mrs. Davis said gently shaking his hand. "Marilyn is almost ready and will be out in just a minute. Can I get you anything to drink?"

"No m'am. But, thank you anyway," Mark replied. "This dinner party is supposed to really be something magnificent. It benefits the Hope Children's Home and several local celebrities are going to be there. I think Marilyn will really enjoy it."

"Of course, she will! Oh, here she is." Even Marilyn's mother was amazed at how pretty she looked after having only a few minutes to get ready.

"Hi, Mark! I hope you didn't mind waiting for me," Marilyn said as she grabbed her purse and light throw.

"You look absolutely beautiful this evening, Marilyn. I will be the envy of all of the other gentlemen at this party, having you on my arm," Mark said as Marilyn slightly blushed and her mother grinned.

"You two have a wonderful time. You'll have to tell me all about it tomorrow." Marilyn's mother let them out the door then retreated to the kitchen. Mr. Davis had just come in from a meeting he had to attend at the local Lions Club.

"What did ya think?" he asked his wife, knowing that Mark had just left with Marilyn.

"Oh, he seems like a really nice, young man. He is handsome and *very* polite. I can just tell you, though, that he can't compete with Brandon. I can see it in Marilyn's eyes. She's really smitten with Brandon."

"Like I said, competition is a good thing-- certainly can't hurt. Since we're not going to any extravagant dinner party tonight, have ya thought about what we might be having for dinner?" He was not unlike any other man---wanting to know what he was going to eat.

"Why don't we do something different tonight, honey?" Mrs. Davis asked her husband.

"Why don't we go to The Riverside Café and have catfish. It's all you can eat tonight. We haven't done that in a long time."

"I can handle that. But don't let me eat 'all you can eat' will ya?" he replied. He had always had a slim physique but with every year, his middle grew a little larger. Now he knew he needed to lose a little weigh--but he absolutely loved to eat! It was one of his pleasures in life.

Mrs. Davis grabbed her purse, and the two of them were out the door. It was a very short drive to the café and the evening air was cool. It was always fun seeing the other townspeople who were at the café. They really didn't know many people, yet, since they hadn't lived in the town very long, but some of the faces seemed familiar. They were seated in a booth near the back of the café. It was really pretty busy for a Friday night, so most of the booths and tables were full. As the Davises were reading through the menu, trying to decide if they were going to have the catfish or something else, a group of young men were being seated in the booth next to theirs. Because the young men were so close, it was quite easy to hear their conversation.

"There's a new girl in town for the summer," one of the guys said with authority. "I hear that she is really beautiful and really smart."

"And if she IS smart then you wouldn't have a chance with her, don't ya know?" his friend said to him with a chuckle.

"Well, you never know. She's just a little younger than we are, so she might think we are pretty-hot stuff," the first voice said. "You guys hang back and watch what happens. I have a real gift with college girls." The boys just laughed and continued to joke with one another. The Davises got a kick out of the conversation. They didn't know for sure that the boys were talking about Marilyn but the description seemed to fit. They knew that if the boys WERE talking about Marilyn, none of them would have a prayer with her. She was already pretty smitten with Brandon and even Mark was going to find that out soon enough.

Mark was the perfect gentleman, holding Marilyn's arm in case she stumbled on the steps, and then opening her car door and helping her in the car. The short trip to Brookhollow Country Club was very pleasant. Mark and Marilyn talked about the celebrities who were supposed to be in attendance. Marilyn knew most of them since they were well known in the community as well as in the surrounding towns. There were going to be local theater personalities, radio news announcers, the mayor, councilmen, society women, and such. Marilyn had never been enamored by society personalities. She was more interested in her family and her church members. She wasn't even excited with movie stars. Nonetheless, Marilyn acted interested since Mark was, and decided to just see how the evening went.

When Mark and Marilyn pulled up to the circular drive where the valet-parking stand was sitting, they could also see several newspaper reporters followed by their photographers. Flash bulbs were going off every few seconds as they hustled to capture pictures of the guests as they entered the club. Just as Marilyn was assisted out of the car by the valet, and Mark joined her taking her arm, a flash went off in their faces. They saw stars for a few seconds--- the flashbulbs were so blinding. Once inside, the same thing happened. Several times pictures were taken of them, usually Mark was holding Marilyn closely with his head tilted towards hers. Marilyn did not think about it at the time, but the couple's picture was going to be on the front page of the local newspaper, the <u>Slatonite.</u>

Inside, the couple was greeted by many of Mark's friends who were social pillars in the community. Mark introduced Marilyn around the crowd very proudly. No one had seen Mark with a young lady in quite some time and they found it refreshing.

Mark and Marilyn were seated near the front of the ballroom. They were able to see the speaker perfectly. The tables were elegantly draped and topped with wonderful floral arrangements as centerpieces. The china and silver were simply elegant. After socializing with everyone at the table, Marilyn finally had one moment to think about Brandon. She wondered what he was doing. She wondered what he was thinking. She couldn't wait until the following evening when she would be with him at the ballet. She really wanted to close her eyes, wave some magic wand, and then "poof!" she would be with Brandon on their way to the ballet. She then realized she would be just as excited if it were the park instead of the ballet. It wasn't the activity or location---it was Brandon.

"Do you need anything?" Mark asked Marilyn as the crowd's noise diminished to a low hum.

"No, thank you. I am doing just fine," Marilyn answered realizing that she must have looked like she was daydreaming. She decided she must tune in to the evening and stop thinking about Brandon just this once.

The evening was delightful. The food was wonderful and the conversation was interesting. The crowd applauded the presentations that were made. The dinner was deemed to be a complete success with their goal for donations to the children's home met. Mark and Marilyn talked about the event all the way home.

"Here we are," Mark said as he pulled up to the Davis home. "Thank you so much for honoring me with your presence tonight."

"No, thank YOU." Marilyn responded. "I had a delightful time and it was everything you said it would be!"

"Marilyn, may I call you again sometime?"

Marilyn found herself in the same predicament that she was in when Mark asked her to go to the dinner. She thought he was a perfect gentleman, but she was still enamored with Brandon. She wondered what she should say. She should have thought this all out before she left that evening, but she hadn't.

"Sure," she responded without wanting to respond.

"Great! That's wonderful! I'll be out of town for about two weeks on a special business that I have to go on, but I'll call you the minut back in town. Is that a deal?"

Totally relieved, Marilyn was able to ans

more cheerful tone. "It's a deal." Marilyn knew that she would not have to think about what to do for a whole two weeks. *Ah! No problem.* At least that is what she thought.

Mark walked her to the door, told her again how much he enjoyed her company, and waved as he turned and walked back down the sidewalk to his car. Marilyn shut the door and walked to her room. She was tired but also felt that the sooner she got to sleep, the sooner she would wake up and it would be Saturday. She couldn't wait. She wanted to go to sleep now---and dream of Brandon.

12

Marilyn woke up to the cheerful singing of the birds that were residents of the trees around the house. She knew for sure that one of them was a mockingbird but there were also a few doves. She loved hearing the gentle cooing sound of the doves. She was in an overall great mood and knew exactly why. Jumping out of bed, she ran to the kitchen and started breakfast before her mother could even get there. Marilyn wanted to start frying the bacon and brewing the coffee. Why should her mother always have the responsibility of cooking breakfast? Since Marilyn was there for the summer, she could help her mother out by at least cooking breakfast whenever possible.

"My, oh my!" her mother said as she walked into the kitchen in her worn, pink house shoes and robe. "I don't know if I can take this. And, don't get me too use to this. I won't let you go back to college in the fall!"

Marilyn smiled as she poured her mother a cup of coffee. She hoped that it tasted good. Marilyn didn't drink coffee so she never knew for sure if she made it to her mother's taste.

"Mom, I could never do enough for you. I owe you everything, so let me do these little things whenever I can. By the way, how does the coffee taste? Too strong?" Marilyn asked sincerely. "It looks a little dark."

"It is the best coffee I've had served to me *ever*!" her mother cheerfully responded with emphasis on the 'ever.'

As they sat down waiting for her father to appear, Marilyn's mother asked her about dinner the night before. Her mother already knew the analysis. It was a great evening, with great conversation, and great food, but there was one thing missing. Brandon.

"I had a nice time with Mark. The dinner was really nice and the organizers met their goal in contributions for the children's home. We certainly saw a lot of well known people there and everyone seemed to know Mark. He wants to ask me out again, but he's going to be out of town for the next two weeks," Marilyn said.

"And why do I think that you were relieved to hear that?" her mother asked.

"That would be because you know me well, I'm guessing." Marilyn couldn't help but smile. Her mother knew that she did *not* want to hurt Mark's feelings or reject him, but at the same time she didn't really want to complicate her life by having two men asking her out, especially when she was so crazy about one of them.

Marilyn finished breakfast and then ran back to the library to finish the research she needed for the article she was writing. This time, she wouldn't wait to the last minute to rush home and get ready for the evening. This time, she would start at least two hours ahead of time, so she could soak in the bubble bath and think about Brandon. She also wanted plenty of time to apply her makeup perfectly, and she wanted plenty of time to put her hair up. Everything had to be perfect this time. Everything.

Marilyn could feel herself getting anxious. She was ready fifteen minutes early and there was nothing she could do to relax those last fifteen minutes. When she finally sat down on the couch instead of pacing on the floor, she had to get up just to check to make sure her slip wasn't showing. Then she had to check her hair to make sure not one curl was out of place. Then she had to make sure her lipstick was the right shade for her face.

"You are beautiful," her father said to Marilyn as her mother began preparing dinner for him.

"You are actually radiant!" her mother exclaimed between peeling the potatoes and rinsing the lettuce. "Try to relax! There is nothing you can do to improve anything! And –no—your slip is not showing."

The last fifteen minutes seemed like an hour. At least the time went by faster when her parents started distracting her.

Knock—knock—knock. The soft knock was heard in the kitchen. Marilyn looked at her mother with eyes wider than normal. It made her parents laugh.

Marilyn went toward the door but twirled around before reaching it. No one saw that. Opening the door, Marilyn exclaimed, "Brandon! *Surely* you knew that I would be right on time tonight!"

"I have asked you before not to call me *Shirley*!" Brandon said seriously while mentally reminding her what he had said in the park. He then broke into a hard laugh. Marilyn couldn't contain herself either. She giggled uncontrollably.

"Listen to that, honey," Mrs. Davis said quietly to her husband in the kitchen. "I love to hear Marilyn laugh like that."

"Bye everybody! We're leaving!" Marilyn yelled from the living room knowing her parents could hear her.

Her parents heard the door shut but they could hear laughter continuing down the sidewalk. Their little girl was going to have a wonderful time and they were happy.

"I am so glad you could change the tickets from Friday night to tonight. I wouldn't want to miss this for anything!" Marilyn said slightly catching herself when she mentioned Friday. She really didn't want to say anything about Friday night.

"Oh, sure. It wasn't that hard. I just had to call my boss's son who originally got the tickets for me, and then I had to call his girlfriend who knew of someone who might have some tickets available for Saturday. Then she asked me to call another friend of hers who happened to know a policeman who couldn't attend the Saturday performance. Unfortunately, he had handed off his tickets to his mother, but she came down sick so she asked me to call the preacher….." Brandon went on and on. Marilyn was actually falling for it until she realized he was just joking. Marilyn burst out laughing.

"So, I owe you? I mean I owe you big time?" She responded jokingly.

"Yep. You owe me big time," he responded. "I'll just have to figure out how you're going to repay me. I think you're going to have to go to the park with me again Sunday evening. Yep! That's it. The park---tomorrow evening around 5:30. You can't get out of it. You owe me."

Marilyn loved every minute of this conversation. In fact, she couldn't keep from smiling. She loved everything about being with Brandon.  Now, if she could just keep the evening from ending so soon. *Please,* she thought.  *Let this last.*

13

Arriving at the performing arts center, Brandon escorted Marilyn to one of the front row seats.  He was so proud to walk her down the long aisle to the row where their seats were located.  Every eye was on him, also.  There were plenty of girls seated who would have loved to be escorted by Brandon and actually, there were plenty of moms seated who would have loved for Brandon to be escorting their daughters.  He was just that respected and well liked.

The lights blinked as a signal for all the people to take their seats.  The lights were dimmed and the music began.  Marilyn couldn't believe she was there.  Here she was in one of the best seats in the house and was sitting next to one of the best, young men in the whole community.  Besides that, she loved ballet, so nothing could be better.  *Let this last,* she thought. *Let this last!*

The music was magnificent.  The costumes were exquisite.  The dancers seemed to float in the air. Marilyn could feel herself sway with the movements on the stage.  She had been in plenty of performances similar to this and longed to be a part of a more professional company where she might begin her career.

At the first intermission, when the house lights were raised, Marilyn could see people looking at them. She was sure everyone wondered what young lady had captured the popular Brandon for the evening. No one really knew who she was.

When the lights dimmed again for the next performance, Brandon reached over to hold Marilyn's hand. She couldn't believe it. She was overcome with the nicest feeling. She didn't even know what happened for the next ten or so minutes. All she could think about was how wonderful Brandon was and how good it felt to be holding his hand.

He felt the same way. The dancers were dancing but his heart was racing. He was taking a big chance by just holding her hand but he rationalized again that holding hands was pretty innocent. Yes---but his feelings were building by the minute. *What if I put my arm around her shoulder? I really want to feel closer to her right now. No—no-not now—too soon!* he discussed with himself.

At the end of the performance, Brandon and Marilyn made their way down the aisle to the back of the hall. Some of the people who were waiting in their seats stared and then whispered among themselves. Again, Marilyn thought that they were just wondering who she was. She did not know it at the time, but they would not have to wonder for very long! The town's newspaper was coming out the next day---and her picture was plastered all over the front page---with Mark----leaning head to head!!

Marilyn didn't want the ride home to end. She really wanted the distance to be much greater than it actually was. In such a short time, Brandon pulled up to the front of the Davis home. "Here we are again---another wonderful evening. I bet you thought I would forget the debt you owe me, though," Brandon said as he walked Marilyn up the front walk. This time he had his arm around her waist. He wanted to pull her close to him but he was content just to just put his arm around her waist. No, that was a lie. He wasn't content. Hell, no. He wanted to pull her close to his body and hold her in his arms. He wanted to take her face in his hands and pull her lips to his. He envisioned a long, passionate kiss. *But no---no—not now---be patient. Don't blow it!*

"You mean the walk to the park tomorrow evening?" she responded. "I know it is something that I don't want to do and I know it is going to be difficult, but I always pay my debts and if I have to do it, I just have to do it." Her eyes twinkled and caught the light from the moon.

They both laughed so hard that Marilyn's parents could hear the laughter from inside their bedroom.
"They certainly laugh a lot, don't they? her father stated.

"Yes—isn't that nice," her mother responded pleasantly.

Brandon thanked Marilyn again for going with him and then there was a really long pause. He stared into her eyes and he wanted to say so much. He wanted to tell her how he had never thought about a girl the way he thought about her. He wanted to tell her that he had such a physical attraction to her that he was afraid to get very close to her. He wanted to tell her that he couldn't even get his work done because he thought about her all the time. Without a word, and with just eye contact, Marilyn seemed to fully understand. And then he turned to leave. Marilyn shut the door and paused briefly. Her wonderful evening was over, but now she could look forward to the walk in the park tomorrow. *"Perfect,"* she thought.

15

Bright and early the next morning, the local newspaper boys threw the newspaper to almost every home in the community. The Slatonite was a small, community newspaper filled with the usual items of interest for a small town. There was always something interesting going on in the town and there were always reports and photographers to cover the events.

Coach Jones always wrote a small article about the local, high school-sports teams since he was Slaton's athletic director and his sports writer/photographer, Kevin, made sure he made it to all the football, basketball, and volleyball games. He was the best at capturing the action shots, especially the ones that made the home teams look the best. Angela was the specialist for all the engagements and weddings. She didn't have to take the pictures since the brides usually had one they wanted to contribute. Unfortunately, Angela was also in charge of collecting and writing obituaries. She was wonderful at it, but she preferred weddings to funerals. Orvil had the most varied job at the newspaper. He covered real news---the events that were worthy of mentioning on the front page. And that is exactly where the Hope Children's Home Charity Dinner made news---on the front page!

"Marilyn, guess whose picture is right on the front page?" her mother asked as Marilyn entered the kitchen the next morning. Marilyn ran over to the table where he mother had the front page smoothed out on the top of the table.

"Oh, no!" Marilyn exclaimed remembering those blasted photographers who took a million pictures at the children's home benefit dinner on Friday night. "Please say it isn't so!" she exclaimed with a grimace on her face. Marilyn really didn't want Brandon to see the picture and the topic of conversation never came up the night before. Now Brandon is going to know why she couldn't go with him Friday night!

"Your dad said a little competition is good, so maybe this is a good thing," Marilyn's mother commented.

"I just think the world of Brandon and I don't want him to get the wrong idea about Mark. At least Brandon and I are going to the park again tonight, so I'll see if he brings the subject up."

"I'm not a betting person, but I would have to say that it'll definitely come up."

Marilyn signed pretty heavily and held up the paper so she could see the picture more clearly. Right there in the middle of the front page was the picture of Mark and Marilyn with the biggest smiles on their faces. They looked like they were having the grandest of times.

The whole idea depressed Marilyn. She was so high after her glorious evening with Brandon and now she was depressed that the picture had come out in the paper. She knew Brandon would see it and she was so afraid of what he might think. At least she'd see him again tonight. Knowing she'd see him soon did not change the fact that she was worried about it.

"We need to go to church a little earlier this morning," Mr. Davis said as he adjusted his tie and then sat down at the breakfast table. "I told Mrs. Bernett that we'd pick her up on the way. She doesn't have a ride this morning."

"Mrs. Bernett? Is that Mark's mother?" Marilyn asked.

"Yes, it is," he answered.

*Oh, gee. Is this awkward?* Marilyn wondered to herself.

Marilyn had no objections. Her father was always helping someone out, but Mark's mother? She wondered if Mark's mother had seen the picture, yet, and if she'd say anything about it. Mr. Davis drove up to the house in the cul-de-sac on Waggoner Drive and walked up the sidewalk to get Mrs. Bernett. She was ready and looked lovely in her Sunday church attire. Upon entering the car, she leaned over to Marilyn and said, "It's such a pleasure meeting you. I've heard wonderful things about you from my son, Mark. He said the two of you had a wonderful time at the dinner the other night."

"Yes, we had a great time. Everything was beautiful," Marilyn responded politely.

"Well, you're just as beautiful as Mark said you were."

Marilyn smiled and thanked Mrs. Bernett for the compliment.

Just as the car crossed the intersection at the corner of the church, Marilyn spotted Brandon. He was standing on the corner ready to cross the street. He recognized the Davis car, smiled as he waved to them, paused for a second as his eyes scanned the occupants in the car, then proceeded to enter the church. Marilyn wondered if he knew who Mrs. Bernett was----whose mother she was. *Well, of course, he did. He knew everyone.* She just couldn't worry about what Brandon might think---or, really she could. Needless to say, her mind wandered throughout the entire sermon. She heard a few things the preacher said, but she was mainly thinking about what Brandon would say about the picture on the front page of the paper. After church, they drove Mrs. Bernett back to her house on the beautiful tree-lined street. She thanked them sincerely.

"Thank you again for taking me to church. I really didn't want to miss today. And what a pleasure meeting you, Marilyn! You are everything Mark said you were and more!" Mrs. Bernett said, affectionately patting Marilyn on her shoulder. Mr. Davis walked her to her front door and helped her in before returning to the car. Marilyn couldn't wait for 5:30 to come. *Funny,* she thought. *When I'm with Brandon, I don't want the time to pass at all; when I'm not with him, it can't pass fast enough.*

## 16

At 5:30 sharp, Brandon knocked on the door. Marilyn was already ready and was watching out the window when he drove up.

Opening the door, Brandon was the first one to speak. "OK, I am here to collect my debt. Are you ready to go?" Brandon looked extremely handsome this particular evening. His eyes sparkled as he spoke and his smile was radiant.

"Do I really have to? *Surely* someone else would be better at this than me!" Marilyn said with a frown on her face until she could no longer pretend. Then she burst out laughing.

"I don't know how many times I have to remind you that my name is not *Shirley*. No, nobody else will do. You have to go with me."

Both laughed again as they walked down the street toward the park. Nothing was said about the newspaper. Perhaps Brandon was too busy to see the paper this morning. As Marilyn tried to figure out all the scenarios that were possible, she decided that the best action was to mention something about it once they reached the park. Brandon did not wait that long. Just as they reached the park he said, "Great picture of you in the paper this morning!"

"Oh, I can't believe they really took that picture!"

"Guess that's why you couldn't go to the ballet on Friday night?" Brandon tried to make it sound like he was kidding around with her, but he was really just a little jealous of the whole situation.

"Yes, I feel really terrible about that. I got myself into a situation that I couldn't get out of. I am sorry."

"Hey! There is no need to apologize to me! You are a very beautiful and brilliant woman. There will be dozens of men knocking at your door. I just happen to be the one who is going to knock the most often and the loudest. I want to see you every chance I can possibly get. I hope you feel the same way about me."

"I certainly do! I have never felt as good as I feel when I am with you. We always have so much fun together."

"Marilyn, you make me happy. I'm more cheerful when I'm around you. I laugh a lot more when I'm around you. I realize your parents probably want you to date other men before you eventually settle down and I'm willing to be patient. If you have to see other people, then do that, but please save some time for me."

"Brandon, I'm really not interested in anyone else. I must go where my heart takes me. Brandon, my heart takes me to you."

17

Brandon and Marilyn spent every evening together for the next ten days. They went to the park, went out to dinner, drove around town, and attended church together. When they discovered how much each other loved to dance, that became their activity of choice. Dances were held every Friday and Saturday night at the VFW Hall on Main Street downtown. The bands that played there always played a variety of music. Sometimes they played western music so Brandon taught Marilyn how to do the Two-Step and the Cotton-eyed Joe. Sometimes they played waltzes and other classical pieces. Brandon could see how much Marilyn floated across the dance floor. Together they were magnificent. In fact, Marilyn told Brandon that she didn't know what she'd do without dancing in her life---she loved it that much. What she meant but didn't say was how she didn't know what she'd do without *Brandon* and dancing in her life.

After spending so much time together, Brandon knew that he wanted to secure their relationship further, and he wasn't going to take any chances. He didn't believe Marilyn was interested in Mark. He also knew that Mark had been gone on a business trip for about two weeks. On the night before Mark was to return, Brandon had a serious conversation with Marilyn.

"Marilyn," Brandon said with the most serious look on his face. "Marilyn, I need to talk to you about something." They were sitting in Marilyn's living room after having dinner at the cheerleaders' spaghetti supper at the high school.

Without mentioning a word about Mark or the homework assignment Brandon had given himself on the topic, he proceeded with the following oratory.

"Marilyn, you must know that I enjoy you very, very much. No one has ever made me feel the way that you do. You make me smile. You make me laugh. I don't want to go anywhere or do anything without you. I know this is rather sudden, but I can't hide the way I feel. I know I said I'd still be around if you wanted to sometimes see other people, but the reality is that I don't want you to. Do you think your parents would possibly approve of us having an exclusive relationship?"

Marilyn just stared at him for a second. She had never seen him be so serious. Before she could say anything, Brandon continued.

"I know you will be going back to college in the fall, but could we at least have an exclusive relationship until you leave? And, by the way, I can't even talk about your leaving in the fall. Not now. I can't even think about it." He shook his head from side to side. Marilyn thought she detected a tear in his eye.

Marilyn felt overcome with emotion. Tears swelled up in her eyes. She was overwhelmed with happiness and could think of nothing that would make her happier. Brandon stared at her not knowing what to think.

"Darling, Brandon," Marilyn said wiping the tears from her eyes. "I would love to have an exclusive relationship with you. You make me so very happy. I was hoping it could be that way."

"What about your parents?"

"Somehow I think they will understand. I really do."

With that, Brandon leaned over and gently nestled Marilyn's face in his hands. He wiped the tears that were still on her face and then gently stroked her hair to smooth it. He leaned close and gently kissed her lips. Marilyn sat there, wanting to freeze the moment in time forever.

Without saying another word, Brandon let himself out of the front door and ran to his car. Marilyn was still in shock. She sat motionless for several minutes before retiring to her bedroom. Getting ready for bed, she replayed the kiss over and over again in her mind. She slowly drifted off to sleep, dreaming about Brandon—and the kiss.

Marilyn's parents were still awake when they heard Brandon leave the house.

"Think about it," Mr. Davis said to his wife. "With as much time as they're spending together, either they'll get tired of each other, or they'll determine they can't be without each other. It'll work out for the best---always does."

"What do you think will happen when Marilyn goes back to college?" his wife asked. "It's pretty hard to keep a relationship going long distance. I know Marilyn is going to miss him desperately. I just hope she can keep her mind on her schoolwork enough to finish out her senior year. Many a young girl has quit to get married-- only to regret it later."

According to Mr. Davis, things would work out.

18

The next morning, Marilyn bounced out of bed in her usually cheerful fashion and danced to the kitchen. Her fuzzy house slippers weren't as conducive to her ballet twirls and pirouettes as her ballet shoes were, but that never held Marilyn back. Her mother was just sitting down at the table to wait for her biscuits to brown a little further.

"Mom, Brandon and I talked about---I guess you could say---going steady. Do you think Dad would approve?" Marilyn always had a few minutes to talk to her mother before her father came to breakfast.

"Marilyn, you're an intelligent young woman. You're twenty years old and almost a college graduate. I think you should make the decision for yourself based on how you feel. I think your dad will respect your decision. Neither your dad nor I want anything to come in the way of your finishing college. If you can go steady with Brandon and still graduate on time, I think your father will approve."

Marilyn felt relieved at her mother's answer. She wondered if there were ever a day in her entire life when she was happier than she was now. Although she never said it out loud, Marilyn knew that she was falling in love---no---had fallen in love with Brandon. Her parents knew that, too.

Brandon and Marilyn dated exclusively throughout June, July, and August. Neither spoke of the day that Marilyn would have to return to school, a location over four hours away. Somehow, they both felt that if they didn't talk about it, the time would never come. Neither could imagine not being together every day.

One might think that they could see each other on the weekends but that would be difficult also. Marilyn was involved in musical performances and dance performances almost every weekend. That was the downside of majoring in music and being a talented dancer. If Brandon drove to see her performance, he would have to drive back home after it was over----a four-hour drive to return, or stay in a small hotel there overnight. They would definitely see each other. They would just have to figure out how to do it.

In the meantime, Marilyn didn't have to worry about Mark asking her out. Brandon made sure, with the help of a few good friends, that Mark heard that they were dating exclusively. In fact, it was only a matter of days and the entire town knew that Marilyn and Brandon were going steady. There were many disappointed young women in town, but there was one really, really happy one. That is all that mattered to Brandon.

Marilyn's parents came to love Brandon as much as Marilyn did. They couldn't find one thing about Brandon that they would change. Several times they discussed their desire for Marilyn to complete her degree and Brandon assured them that she would graduate on time.

On the evening before Marilyn was to return to school, Brandon held Marilyn in his arms and said, "Marilyn, I feel like my heart is being torn from my body. I love you. I love you with all my heart." Brandon had never told Marilyn that he loved her until now. They both seemed to know it, but neither had actually said the words.

Brandon continued, "I'll do whatever I have to do to see you. I promised your parents that you would graduate, and you are too close not to do that. If that means that I see you only on some weekends, then it will have to be that way. If I can only see you from a seat in the audience at one of your performances, then that's what I'll do. You don't know how important you are to me."

Marilyn responded, "Brandon, my darling, I'd gladly give up my degree to stay with you. I love you more than you know. You are the reason I live and breathe. How can I continue without you?"

"It'll be hard on both of us, but we are strong. You'll be busy with all of your schoolwork and all of your performances. I'll be busy with the office work and community service. And during all of this, we'll write. You'll be right here in my heart---you'll go with me everywhere." Brandon held her hand to his chest and then kissed her goodnight. He turned to walk away.

## Chapter Three
## Long Distance Romance

The next day came and Marilyn had to head back to school. Brandon was right there to see her off. He slipped a small envelope into her purse and told her not to open it until she got back to her dorm room.

Marilyn threw her arms around her father, then her mother, then Brandon, giving them a long, sincere hug to say good-bye. Her parents stood next to Brandon as they each waved---her car slowly heading down the road. They couldn't see the tears that were streaming down Marilyn's face. She cried most of the way back to the campus. Even her parents worried how Marilyn was going to do without Brandon.

"I know she is heartbroken for having to leave you, Brandon," Mrs. Davis said with heartfelt sympathy. "But, you'll still get to see one another, not as often as you've grown accustomed to, but you'll see, like her father says, it <u>will</u> all work out."

"Yes, I'm heartbroken, but I know how important it is to both of you that she finish and graduate. I promise you I'll not stand in her way. I'll help anyway that I can. That's my word to you," Brandon said with conviction.

The Davises knew that he meant it. They knew that he would miss Marilyn, too. Waiting wasn't going to be easy for him, either.

Sometimes, it's the young whose feelings of love are so intense. When they fall in love, the feelings are so strong that they overpower everything else. Brandon and Marilyn had never experienced that feeling before, but they were experiencing it now. It was a beautiful----a very beautiful feeling.

Pulling into the campus, Marilyn glanced around at the towering trees, the red brick dormitories with white wood trim, and the winding trails of sidewalks branching out to the various buildings. She thought it strange that she did not have the usual feeling of excitement at starting a new year at the university. She had always been so anxious to see what classes she would get, what professors she would have, and what activities would fill her days and nights. She was always in the midst of the activity, being one of the most popular young ladies on campus.

This time, the return to the university campus was not the same as it had been in previous years after her summer break. In the past, Marilyn was always anxious to return---she loved the campus activity and seeing her many friends. She noticed the hustle and bustle of the new students on campus and the parents helping their children with items for their dorms. She waved to a few of her friends who shared the same dorm with her. She still felt sad. *Funny what falling in love will do to you. It alters the way you view everything. Your life is really changed forever.*

Marilyn tried to pat some powder on her face to

conceal the fact that she had been crying all the way there. Sunglasses would help, she thought. A few boxes, and she would have a new residence. It certainly wasn't the sun-filled room that she had at her parents' home, but it would do for now. She thought back to the floral window treatments and bedspread that her mother had carefully sewn for her. The new additions made her room seem like a flower garden blooming in the early spring. She would try to go home as often as she could, although her schedule was usually pretty hectic during the school year. Now she had more of a reason than ever. She was in love with Brandon--- deeply in love with Brandon.

Most of the other girls had already moved into their dorm rooms. They moved in two or three days earlier. Marilyn had done that in the past. This year, however, she waited as late as she could in order to spend more time with Brandon. She figured she could throw her clothes in the drawers, make the bed, and be ready for class the next morning. She would have to run down to pick up her official schedule but could do that in the afternoon.

This was going to be a long semester. Somehow, if she could just make it to Thanksgiving, she would have a nice break and could return home for a few days. Then if she could make it to Christmas, she would have a break of about a month. Even though there would be Christmas performances in which to participate, everything pretty much stopped by the second week in December. Marilyn mapped out as much as she could on the calendar, noting which weekends she could be back in Slaton. Then she remembered the envelope that Brandon gave her as she was left home. He told her not to open it until she got to her dorm room, so she basically forgot about it until this minute. Opening her purse, she shuffled through various items until she saw the envelope. Tearing it open, she found a beautiful card with red and yellow roses on the front. Brandon knew the Marilyn loved roses and would often call her 'Rosebud' as a term of endearment. Opening the card, she found a letter. She read:

*My Dearest Marilyn,*

*It's with great sadness that I write this letter, knowing that you're leaving me to return to the university today. I want to hold onto you and tell you that I'll never let you go. After you came into my life, the sun now shines brighter, the grass grows greener, and the flowers are all so much more beautiful. Thinking about you brings feelings of great joy and happiness. I love our laughter. You are the most beautiful girl that I 've ever seen, but you're just as beautiful on the inside as you are on the outside. If I could paint the perfect woman and describe a perfect personality, the picture I'd paint would be of you and the description I'd write would be you. Marilyn, please work hard while at school, and promise to come back to me as often as you possibly can. I can't wait until we can be together again.*

> *With heart felt love,*
> *Brandon*

Marilyn melted as she read the letter. Again, tears softly trickled down her cheeks. She carefully folded the letter and placed it back in the card. She slid the card back into the envelope. She didn't notice until then that Brandon had addressed the envelope to "Rosebud." She smiled. The envelope would go in the bottom of the top drawer, a handy place for retrieving it when she wanted to read it again. Marilyn didn't know it then, but she would read that letter many, many times over the next few months.

After Brandon left the Davis house, he drove very slowly to the edge of the park that he and Marilyn had visited numerous times over the summer. He just needed some time to himself before going back home. He needed to think about the situation and how he would handle her absence. Thinking of Marilyn brought tears to his eyes. He tried to open his eyes wide and then blink repeatedly, but the tears wouldn't disappear. Finally, he took the handkerchief from his pocket and dabbed his eyes. *Enough of that!* he thought. He needed to take control of his feelings. He didn't understand how his feelings for her could be so strong after only four months, but he couldn't deny them.

After an hour had elapsed, Brandon felt it was time to head back to his house. Bonnie and his parents would be there and he knew they'd want to know how the sendoff went. Actually, they knew how difficult it was for him so they didn't bring it up. They figured if he wanted to talk about it, he would.

"Marilyn's on her way back to college,"

Brandon blurted out to the group waiting in the living room. "It'll probably be a few weeks before she can come back this direction."

"There's nothing that says you can't drive to the university, either," Bonnie mentioned.

"Oh, of course not. I'm sure I'll be doing some of that. It's just that she'll be so darn busy with her senior year and all of the musical performances that she'll be in. I won't miss any of those if I can help it, but it's not like she'll be able to spend much time with me when I go. She'll be rehearsing most evenings. I don't care as long as I get to at least see her," Brandon offered.

Brandon' office wasn't the same either. He once looked forward to getting up each morning, driving to work and interacting with all of his clients. He continued to be the most gracious professional that he'd always been, but he just found it to be very difficult to concentrate on what he was doing. His mind kept flashing back to the times that he spent with Marilyn. His office workers probably thought he was daydreaming more than usual. He was--- dreaming about Marilyn.

He looked at the calendar that hung on his wall by the desk. Just how long was it until Thanksgiving? He counted almost 80 days. Eighty days until Marilyn could come back to Slaton to stay for a few days! Brandon thought that it sounded like an eternity. In the meantime, she would drive down for the weekend whenever possible and he would drive up there to see her performances and steal a little of her time.  If he could just make it to Thanksgiving, then making it to Christmas wouldn't be nearly as difficult.  There would be only three weeks in between.  Marilyn would be home for almost one month in December.  Brandon decided that December was now his favorite month of the year.

Brandon thought about the hug that Marilyn gave him right before she left.  He tried to relive that feeling over and over again.  Then he thought about the envelope that he slipped into her purse.  By now, she would have arrived at the campus, and hopefully, she would have already read the letter.  He wanted to say so many more things to her and would, but for now, that letter would be a start.  He wrote to her frequently, to remind her of his love for her.  He had never been one to write letters but everything in his life seemed to be changing.  He never wanted to settle down with one girl before, but now his heart told him she was the one that he wanted to spend the rest of his life with.  He figured that by the time she graduated, he would be 27 and she would be 21.  He felt that was the perfect age to get married and find a place of his own.  He never wanted his thought of her to end, but the work was piling up on his desk.  He hadn't had a chance to go through his mail in several days, so he had to do that immediately.  After all, if he asked Marilyn to marry him someday, he had to support them.  He had to work---not dream!

2

Marilyn's first day at school was not the same as it had always been before, either. In the past, she was so excited to meet all of the new students who were coming onto the campus. In fact, in the past, she was on the new-student welcoming committee and was responsible of acclimating them to the campus. This year was different. She wasn't on the welcoming committee and wasn't going to be as involved with the underclassman since she was entering her senior year.

Carrie was in Marilyn's first class. She was one of Marilyn's best friends. They met when both girls were freshmen. Both girls were music majors and both loved singing and dancing. They were participants in the same musicals, and they confided in each other like best friends do. They hadn't spoken over the summer since both girls went home to be with their families, who lived several hours apart. It was always fun to catch up with what each other had done when they returned to campus each fall. Marilyn caught a glimpse of Carrie just as she walked through the door. Smiling from ear to ear, Marilyn grabbed Carrie by her shoulders.

"Carrie! You look great! You must've had a restful summer! And your short haircut is beautiful!" Marilyn couldn't help but hug Carrie at that point.

Carrie hugged her, then pushed back to say, "Well, look at you! You look wonderful! What did ya do over the summer? Do I detect a glimmer in your eyes?" Carrie knew something had happened. Marilyn didn't have a new haircut, she was still as svelte as before, but there was something different that Carrie couldn't put her finger on. Carrie could detect an overall radiance.

With the biggest smile on her face, Marilyn said, "I fell in love over the summer. I really fell in love! Can you believe it? I can't! I just can't believe it!"

Both girls squealed and giggled at the same time.

"You have to tell me ALL about him. I want to know every detail. How did ya meet? Where did ya meet? What do your parents think about this? What is his family like? Have you met them? What does he do?" Carrie couldn't get the questions out fast enough.

The girls agreed to meet that afternoon to talk about it. Being the first day of class they wouldn't have any studying to do. Marilyn and Carrie met at the Student Union Center that afternoon around 3:00 p.m. Finding a small table in a private area of the room, the girls sat sipping on soft drinks they had just purchased.

"I can't wait to hear all about this, Marilyn. Please take your time and try to remember every detail. This is better than reading a good book!"

"I can't believe it myself. I still can't believe it. I just hope I don't wake up to find out that it was actually just a dream," Marilyn said.

Marilyn began at the very beginning, just as Carrie wanted, careful not to leave out anything. Carrie listened intently with her eyes fixed on Marilyn's eyes the entire time. When Marilyn smiled, Carrie smiled. When Marilyn's expression looked serious, Carrie followed with the same. By the end of the story, Carrie and Marilyn were both crying. Then Marilyn pulled out the letter that Brandon had given her as she left home and let Carrie read it.

After reading the letter, she said, "You have to go back to him. This is something really very special. Love like this just doesn't come along every day, Marilyn. Some people don't find love like this in a whole lifetime! Go, Marilyn----go back to Brandon!"

"Carrie, you have to help me. I *have* to finish my degree. I promised my parents and Brandon gave his word to that also," she begged her best friend.

"OK, we can do this. I'll help you." Carrie was the most supportive friend Marilyn could have ever hoped to have.

The time had disappeared. The girls were so engaged in the story that time passed without them even knowing. It was almost seven o'clock! It was very therapeutic for Marilyn to talk to Carrie. Talking about it seemed to help Marilyn get a grasp on the situation. Marilyn vowed to Carrier to work hard in school, to keep the relationship going with Brandon by writing letters and visiting him whenever possible, and to graduate next May. Carrier would help her get through the next nine months.

The girls hugged each other again, then walked

back to their dorm.  Marilyn dropped by the bookstore to buy some stationery.  She would go through two boxes before she switched to notebook paper.  The stationery was fine for short letters, but Marilyn's were of greater length.  She needed notebook paper for her class work anyway.

Writing letters to Brandon was also therapeutic for Marilyn.  It made her feel like she had a closer connection to him, and it was particularly nice when she received letters from him, also.

She also figured out that her professors wouldn't know she wasn't taking notes in their class if she handled it the right way.  Her writing would look like she was taking notes of the lectures, but, in fact, Marilyn would be writing letters to Brandon.  Occasionally, Marilyn would look up at the professor and nod.  She would be really quite good at listening to the lecture at the same time she would write letters to Brandon. She had it all figured out.

That night in her dorm room, Marilyn penned her first letter.  She realized this was the first letter she had ever written to Brandon.  Hopefully, she could express herself in writing to convey her true feelings.  After all, she wasn't a writer.

*Dearest Brandon,*

*The card and letter that you gave me yesterday was one that I'll treasure for the rest of my life.  I didn't read it until I got into my room, just as you instructed.  It's the most beautiful card I've ever seen.  You know how much I love rosebuds, don't*

*you! Your letter touched my heart, my darling
Brandon. I just wonder how I'm going to be able to
be away from you without going crazy. I can only
pour myself into my classes so much. Thoughts of
you are with me every minute of every day. If love
is a drop of rain, then my love for you is as big as
the Pacific Ocean.*

*Luckily, one of the first people I saw this morning
was Carrie Williams. She is my best friend.
Remember, I told you about her this summer. She
and I are in the first class together. When she found
out that I had fallen in love this summer, she
insisted on hearing the whole story. We met at the
Student Union Center and I told her everything. In
no time at all, four hours had passed. It was such a
good feeling to talk about our summer and relive
the wonderful times we had.*

*Carrie wanted me to drop out of school
immediately, jump in the car and head home to you
tonight. After I explained what my parents wanted
and how you promised to support me to graduation,
she understood. She's going to take care of me here
and help me finish my studies. I feel like the
luckiest person in the world. I have the most
wonderful parents in the world, I'm in love with the
most fantastic man in the world, and I'm blessed
with a good friend who understands and will
support me. What could be more perfect? I just
pray that the days and weeks speed by quickly.*

*I'll find out the schedule for my musical
performances and will send that to you. Hopefully,
you'll be able to come to at least one of them if your*

*schedule permits. The performances start around the last part of October. I'll keep you in my prayers every night. I love you, Brandon.*

*Love always,*
*Rosebud*

Probably at the same time Marilyn was writing her first letter to Brandon, he was also sitting at his desk writing her a letter:

*Dearest Rosebud,*

*I hope you didn't forget to read the letter that I slipped into your purse yesterday as you were leaving! I wrote it from the heart. I've never been more truthful about my feelings for you. I know by the time you get this letter you'll be settling into the college life once again. I just hope that you don't settle in so much that you leave memories of our time together behind. You'll be surrounded by many handsome, young, college boys who would give anything to be with you. I know that for sure. I just want you to know that none of them---not ONE of them---could possibly love you as much as I do. In fact, if you collected them all together, their total love could not match my love for you.*

*My days aren't changing that much. I still go to the office, meet with our clients, and attend community functions—without you-- I must add. I still drive by the park and try to relive the time we had there together. I eat at the same restaurants when I have to-- although I am trying to spend many more evening meals with my parents. I walk down the same sidewalks, but you are not by my side. I am not complete without you.*

*I can make this work only because I know we'll be together in the end. We have to be strong for one another. I will pray for us.*
                    *Love always,*
                    *Brandon*

It took a couple of days for the letters to reach their recipients. Marilyn's heart started pounding when the letter was slipped under her door. She could barely contain herself in order to tear open the envelope. Brandon felt the same way when his secretary brought the letter to his office and dropped it in the 'In' box on his desk. Marilyn wanted to send her letters to Brandon at his office address so that he would get them sooner. Otherwise, he would not see his mail until he returned home sometimes very late in the evening. Brandon waited until his secretary left his office before he reached for the letter. After reading the letters, Marilyn placed hers in the top draw of her dresser along with the rosebud card, and Brandon placed his letter in his desk file drawer under 'Personal.'

3

Marilyn had only been gone a few days, but Brandon felt that was long enough. He decided that he would drive to the university on Saturday if Marilyn had time to see him. Although it was very difficult to use the telephone on campus, Brandon decided that he would try it anyway. He didn't think a letter would reach her in time. He understood that in order to place a call to Marilyn, he would have to call the main number at the university. The call would be transferred to the only phone in the dorm, and it would be answered by the housemother. She would then have to walk to Marilyn's dorm room to get her. Brandon tried to figure out the best time to catch Marilyn. He decided to call pretty late, around 9:00 pm, in hopes that she would be in her room.

Brandon placed the call to the university around 9:00 that evening. It worked just as Marilyn said it would. Brandon first spoke to the university operator; his call was then transferred to the dormitory where Marilyn resided. The dorm mother, Mrs. Bryan, answered on the first ring. She was an older woman who had been a dorm mother for many years. She had no family of her own so the girls who came to live in the dorm were her children, she pretended. Because of her weight, she couldn't move very quickly, and climbing the stairs was even more difficult. She was willing to help.

Mrs. Bryan lived her life through her girls. They told her everything that went on in their lives. If they didn't, then someone else would tell her. Somehow, she always knew everything that went on.

"Hold on, please, young man. It will definitely take me a few minutes to go to her room. Don't hang up," the dorm mother said and then placed the receiver down to go get Marilyn. She had to look up the list of occupants to see what dorm room Marilyn occupied.

She walked down the hall to the stairs, climbed up one flight of stairs, and then walked to the end of the hallway. Marilyn's door was closed. That didn't necessarily mean that Marilyn wasn't there, so the dorm mother knocked. Immediately across the hall was a former roommate of Marilyn, and her door was open. Leaning forward to see who was knocking at the door, Marilyn's former roommate, Rita, said, "Sorry, Mrs. Bryan, Marilyn hasn't gotten back from her committee meeting yet. She should've already been here but I guess she's running a little late!" Mrs. Bryan seemed disappointed.

"Well, will you please tell Marilyn that a *very* nice gentleman tried to call her tonight?"

"Sure will," Rita said. She didn't know how important that phone call actually was. Just a few minutes after Miss Bryan had left, Marilyn appeared at her dorm room.

"Hey, Marilyn!" Rita yelled when she heard Marilyn return. "Miss Bryan was just here a few minutes ago to tell you that you had a phone call."

Marilyn ran across the hall asking, "Did she say who it was?" Marilyn appeared to be very excited.

"She said it was some *veeeerrrrry* nice gentleman."

Marilyn's former roommate had barely gotten the word "gentleman" out of her mouth when Marilyn sprinted down the hallway as fast as she could. She literally flew down the stairs and ran the length of the hallway to Miss Bryan's room. Just as she entered the room, she heard Miss Bryan say to the person on the phone, "I'm so sorry. She wasn't in her room but her neighbor said she was expecting her anytime now. The phones are turned off at 9:30 pm so you might try to call back before then." Brandon's heart dropped. He had so hoped to be able to talk to her about Saturday. Besides, he wanted desperately to talk to her. He really needed to hear her voice.

Miss Bryan then noticed Marilyn almost sliding through the door. "Wait----here she is!"

Marilyn took the phone in her hand, still panting from her sprint down the stairs. "Hello?" she said wanting to hear Brandon's voice on the other end of the line.

"Marilyn?" Brandon asked disguising his voice. The connection wasn't that good and there was plenty of static. "This is Detective Shirley. How are you doing?"

"Detective Shirley?" Marilyn asked, quite puzzled by the voice at the other end of the line and confused why a detective would be calling her anyway.

"I told you not to call me *Shirley!*" Brandon could no longer disguise his voice---and burst out laughing. Marilyn knew instantly she had been fooled once again---but she was thrilled that Brandon was on the line.

"OK, now, how are you doing?" Brandon asked lovingly.

"I'm doing great, Brandon.  No, not really, I'm not doing great.  I miss you desperately." Marilyn had to talk in front of Miss Bryan.  She also knew the call had to be short.  Miss Bryan figured out by that conversation that Marilyn was talking to a very important person in her life.  She made a mental note in case there were future calls.

"Marilyn, I can't go another week without seeing you.  I know we'll get used to this after a while and you may think it is silly but I *have* to see you.  I can't wait any longer.  May I see you on Saturday?  I can be there at 8:00 in the morning and we can spend the day together if that is alright with you," Brandon said praying that she would agree.

"I would love that, Brandon! I'll completely clear my calendar and get any work that I have to do done before you come.  I can't wait to see you. This is the best gift that you could possibly give me. I love you."  With that, Marilyn and Brandon said goodbye and the call ended.

"Thank you so much for the phone call, Miss Bryan.  Sorry I wasn't in my room when you got there.  But thanks so much!"

Marilyn didn't even remember walking back to her room. She didn't remember climbing the stairs.  All she could remember was that Brandon was coming on Saturday.  That was day after tomorrow.  She squealed with delight!  It seemed so long since she had left him but, in reality, it had only been four days.

4

It was pitch black when Brandon rolled over to look at the clock on the nightstand beside his bed.  He had to blink a couple of times to clear his eyes enough to read the numbers.  It was almost 3:30 am, and he wanted to leave his house by 4:00 am.  He jumped out of bed, splashed cold water on his face and then turned on the shower.  Brandon was ready to jump in the shower before it was ready for him to do so.  The water was cool, sending shivers throughout his body and goose bumps on his arms.  Then a warm feeling rushed over him as the warm water streamed over his body.  What a beautiful feeling---but one that would have to be short-lived.  He didn't have time to stand in warm comfort any longer.  He had to get dressed and hit the road.  Brandon set out the clothes he was going to wear the night before, knowing that he could think better at that time of the day.  Marilyn loved his light blue cotton shirt; she said it reminded her of the sky, not to mention that it was one of her favorite colors.  His cream-colored slacks were pressed perfectly and hung with only a slight break at his shoes.  He ran a comb through his hair, which was still slightly wet and grabbed a handkerchief from his top drawer.

Brandon left home at 4:00 am so that he could get to the campus around 8:00 am.  He wanted to take Marilyn to breakfast, and he also didn't want to waste one minute of the day. He was dressed to perfection; this was quite typical for him. He wore the freshly starched, blue shirt, open at the neck, and his pair of cream-colored trousers. He made sure his shoes were shined perfectly. He wanted to look his very best for Marilyn.

He packed a basketful of items in the trunk of his car and then was off. The roads were pitch black for the first hour but then the sky started gradually lightening. There were plenty of small deer, raccoons, and opossums that scurried away from the road as Brandon's car sputtered along. Brandon enjoyed seeing the wildlife. He always felt the animals were God's little creatures and were there to give pleasure to man. Brandon felt that every deer he saw was a beautiful thing to behold. He marveled at the graceful way they leapt through the air or how completely still they could remain, with only a slight twitching of their ears or tails. Brandon knew Marilyn loved all animals as well; Brandon and Marilyn had never had a discussion on the topic, but more than once her mother mentioned Marilyn caring for a small squirrel or injured raccoon. She grew up with a mother cat that had a litter of kittens as often as nature would allow. Marilyn loved each tiny kitten tenderly.

Marilyn woke up throughout the night in anticipation of the day ahead. It seemed that she woke every two hours to look at the clock. First it was around 12:00 midnight. Then it was 2:10 am and then 4:15 am. She got up at 6:30 so make sure that she would be ready when Brandon arrived. Marilyn chose a pretty, light-pink dress with a sash that tied around her waist. The neckline was rounded and slightly beaded. She combed her hair at least three times, trying to get her long, wavy hair to fall just right over her ears. Then she decided to add a ribbon in her hair, so she started all over once again. She had painted her fingernails just the night before and her freshly painted toenails would look great with the sandals she was planning to wear.

As usual, she was totally ready with time to spare. It was always that last fifteen or twenty minutes that would continue to drive her crazy. She would stand up, then sit down, then walk to the window, then walk down the hall. She would repeat that process unless she found something to distract her. She decided to read the last letter that Brandon wrote to her. By the time she read the letter and carefully placed it back in her drawer, it was time to meet Brandon downstairs.

Marilyn wanted to run down the stairs and down the hallway, but she didn't want to be out of breath when she saw Brandon. She knew she would be short of breath, anyway, just because of the excitement of seeing him.

When she approached the foyer, she saw Brandon. His back was toward her; he was looking out of the front window. She had never seen him look so handsome! Suddenly that roller coaster feeling hit her stomach. That was the feeling she always got just as the roller coaster was headed down a steep incline. Her stomach filled with butterflies. Marilyn had that same feeling as she walked closer to Brandon.

"Brandon!" she called out--- he instantly spun around on his heels. She ran the last fifteen feet with arms outstretched. He caught her in his arms and spun her around. It was the greatest feeling in the world for both of them. "I'm the happiest girl in the whole wide world!" she said trying to fight back tears of happiness.

"And you are the most beautiful girl in the whole wide world! Let's not waste one minute of time. Come on—let's get out of here." Brandon put his arm around Marilyn's waist and led her to his car. As they walked out the front door and across the drive, Marilyn felt like she was in a dream. She couldn't believe he was actually there with her and that they would have the whole day together. No meetings, no duties, no errands---just the two of them with time to be together.

They headed for the diner that was closest to the campus. The diner was small, but the service was fast. A row of booths lined the windows that overlooked the street. The middle section was made up of small red tables, with wooden legs and padded, cloth-covered chairs. Single seats---stools with no backs---lined the long counter near the back. They were bolted to the floor and couldn't be moved, but they swiveled from side to side.

Brandon and Marilyn were seated in a booth near the far end away from the door. They liked that, also. Being at the back meant more privacy and fewer people walking by. A small, glass, vase sat at the end of the table. A pink, plastic rose and a few twigs of greenery were placed in the vase to welcome anyone sitting there. Brandon ordered his usual breakfast of eggs, ham, toast, and coffee. Marilyn ordered fruit and a cinnamon roll. She always drank orange juice. They talked and talked and laughed and laughed.

"Marilyn?" Brandon said with a twinkle in his eye. "Do ya want to go to the park that's just on the other side of the campus? I don't know if it's as good as the one back home, and I doubt seriously that it has a giant goldfish in it, but it's worth a try. Want to go?"

"I'd love to go there. Too bad we don't have a quilt! We could put it under a tree and just sit there and relax," Marilyn said thinking that they would definitely do that the first weekend she could get back to Slaton.

"How do ya know we don't have a quilt? I might just have one right in the trunk of my car!" Brandon said with a wink of his eye.

"Reeeaallly?" Marilyn said excitedly. What Marilyn didn't know until they got to the park was that Brandon also had a pillow, a bottle of fruity-tasting wine that had been iced down since 4:00 that morning, a bottle of raspberry tea just in case Marilyn didn't like the wine, and plenty of fruit and cheese. He knew that Marilyn didn't really like wine, but if it tasted more like grape juice, she'd enjoy it as if it were. He planned a picnic lunch so they could be alone most of the day.

When they arrived at the park, Brandon picked out a special spot under a huge tree. It was shady, yet they could still see the blue sky and the clouds that so softly floated by. Brandon pulled out a large quilt that had been in his family for many years. In fact, his grandmother had quilted it with her local quilting group. Brandon remembered as a very small child, walking into the bedroom where his grandmother worked on the quilt. He remembered the cloth stretched out with some kind of clamps holding it up from each of the four corners. His grandmother and the other ladies sat in chairs, leaning over and stitching with their shiny needles. Squares---many colorful squares. Brandon grew up with the quilt but didn't know if his grandmother would appreciate him spreading her quilt over the grass. Even then, he thought, she would approve wholeheartedly if she knew Marilyn. She would approve. Brandon had grabbed a pillow off his bed in case Marilyn needed something on which to rest her head.

Marilyn and Brandon spread the large quilt under the tree, took off their shoes, and just stared at each other. The quilt felt soft over the cushion of green grass and felt cool to the touch. Marilyn noticed the beautiful pattern of the multicolored squares. She knew that many hours of work had gone into making the quilt. They couldn't believe they were getting to spend the day together. Before long, they were laughing as they usually did every time they were together.

There was also a small pond a few yards away from where they were resting. They walked hand-in-hand to the edge of the pond. A lazy turtle that was sunning itself on the bank decided they were walking too close to him, so he scooted back to the pond and disappeared beneath the water. Birds chirped in the sky. Squirrels scampered from tree to tree. Other than that, the whole world stood still at this moment. Brandon and Marilyn were together and that was all that mattered.

"Marilyn, do you like it here?" Brandon asked as he felt the cool breeze on his face.

"Yes---but I don't think it really matters where we are. I just like spending time with you. Tell me more about your parents, Brandon. I really enjoy learning about your family."

"Well, my grandparents on my father's side actually came from Norway. I believe they came over not even knowing how to speak English. I still remember my grandmother had a pretty strong accent. They had to work hard all of their lives, and they never really had very much. Their kids---my father and his two brothers and sister-- scattered to all parts of the country, but I do remember visiting them on several occasions. I have some older cousins but several have passed away. My grandparents died when I was relatively young. My other grandparents were from Germany, actually. Melting pot, huh? Anyway, they worked hard also and had three kids. My maternal grandfather died pretty young of a heart attack, but my grandmother lived to be in her nineties. I know my cousins but we were never close after we kids grew up. Now, I only keep up with one of my aunts."

"Marilyn, tell me about your earliest memory," Brandon said. "How far back in your childhood can you actually remember?"

"I don't know how old I was, but I remember several things. Once, my family and I were at the park in our little hometown. I don't know if it was a July 4th picnic or not but it was an event such as that. I remember someone was carrying me around. It wasn't my mother or father but a teenaged girl. There was some kind of little activity where prizes were given. I remember seeing a young girl, maybe 6 or 7, winning a small plastic purse. It would have been a purse for a small doll of some kind. Well, I wanted that purse. I remember crying and crying. The girl who held me tried to calm me down but nothing would work. Finally, either the girl who had won the purse or someone else, a small girl, came up to me to give me the purse. I instantly quit crying. I'm a little embarrassed by the memory. Was I spoiled or what! I guess I was only two or three years old at the time! I wish I knew exactly how old I was."

Brandon listened to the whole story with a smile on his face. "There was another time---I don't know if this was before or after the purse incident, but my brother and I were in our backyard, right out the back door under a tree. My brother dug a small hole as deeply as he could. Actually, it was probably only about twelve to fifteen inches deep at the most. Anyway, he dug the hole with a kitchen spoon. When it looked pretty deep, he put his ear to the hole. He told me he was listening for the devil.

He let me put my ear to the hole. I couldn't hear a thing, but I believed him when he said he could hear the devil. Evidently, my grandmother, who lived next door saw the whole thing through her window. She probably heard the conversation, too, because later I heard her tell my mother something about it."

Brandon had to laugh at this one. "Well," he said, "You were at least digging in the right direction!"

"I can also remember, about that same time, my father teaching my brother how to play the harmonica----although we called it a French harp in those days. My brother sat on the back steps with my dad sitting beside him. I was sitting there, too, so I watched intently. My father used a hand signal to show my brother when to breathe in and when to blow out. At first, my father moved the harmonica in front of my brother's mouth---making sure to hit the right notes for the song. My brother blew out and breathed in according to my father's hand signal. I was mesmerized. I think the song was 'You Are My Sunshine' although I also remember 'Under the Double Eagle.' I can recall that lesson vividly---as if it were yesterday. Today my brother can play the harmonica beautifully. I can't play a lick-----but I'm good at sitting and watching. Ha."

Marilyn seemed to be enjoying herself---- reminiscing about her childhood brought nice memories and Brandon really enjoyed hearing her stories.

"Oh, my gosh!" Marilyn said opening her eyes as widely as she could. "I have another

123

memory that is unbelievable! It really happened, though."

Brandon couldn't wait to hear her story.

"Remember I told you about my family being at the park?" Marilyn said.

"Is this the same park?" Brandon interrupted.

"Actually, yes, it was. It was the only park in town so it had to be!" she answered. "Well, I don't know if it was the same summer or not, but I have another really vivid memory. Again, I was very, very young. My parents parked their new car on the side of the park where everyone was congregating. Sometime during the picnic, my brother led me over to the car. Of course, the doors were unlocked---you even left your house unlocked in those days! He sat behind the wheel and I climbed up into the front passenger seat. I watched while he pushed in the cigarette lighter. After a few seconds, the lighter popped out---a signal that it was ready and hot enough to light the end of a cigarette. Of course, I watched every move my brother made---I always did. He took the cigarette lighter out of the holder in the dashboard and started burning holes into the vinyl seat that was between where we were sitting. One after another, he pushed the cigarette lighter onto the seat, burning the vinyl and leaving perfect circles burned into the seat. I remember seeing four or five circles. He seemed to think it was fun. I remember thinking that it probably wasn't a good thing. That is where the memory ends. I don't remember leaving the car or if someone came to find us. I don't remember any reaction once my dad saw the seat. I don't recall anything. Oh, my gosh! I wonder what my dad did when he saw that!"

"It's a good thing you didn't take after your brother!" Brandon said with a laugh. "And you say he is really a good guy now?"

"Model citizen," Marilyn replied with a laugh. "Those are my earliest memories. I have many more, but I was older, of course. It's funny to think back on those things."

"Tell me more," Brandon said, partly because he loved to hear Marilyn tell stories and partly because he didn't want the day to end. If she kept telling stories, maybe it would never end.

"I remember I used to get terrible earaches when I was a child. It was so windy where I grew up and, of course, I played outside all of the time. I was a real tomboy." Marilyn started to go on, but Brandon interrupted.

"You were a tomboy? You----with golden curls and flowers in your hair? A tomboy?" Brandon acted totally amazed at the thought.

"Yes—definitely. In fact, I was very proud of the fact that I didn't wear a dress to school for two straight years. I had to wear a dress to church, but I always wore pants to school. *That* was being a tomboy."

Brandon had a look of disbelief on his face. "Go on," he said.

"Well, back to the earaches. I remember getting terrible earaches *every* time I played out in the wind. I remember getting a horrible earache right at Christmas time. When I raised my head up off the pillow, a terrible, yellow liquid ran out of my ear onto the pillowcase. It also sounded like Niagra Falls was in my ear. My dad took me to Dr. Jaynes the next day. Dr. Jaynes looked into my right ear with his instrument and then told my father to look also. "See the hole in her eardrum? She'll need some penicillin to fix this," the doctor said. He gave me a shot (I abhorred needles in those days) and I had to go back for two additional shots. After my eardrum healed, I never had another earache---- not for the rest of my life. That penicillin really worked!"

Marilyn leaned over and hugged Brandon gently as if to thank him for listening to her. Then, she abruptly straightened up and said," Oh no----- another memory----not good. Ya want to hear it?"

"Of course," Brandon said, "Are you kidding! Tell me more."

"Well, when I was very young---must have been only three or four years old---my brother and I were in my grandmother's kitchen. All of the adults were sitting in the living room, talking and laughing. As usual, I followed my brother and watched every move he made out of total curiosity.

126

Of course, I did!  He was always doing something!  Remember the cigarette lighter?  Well, anyway, he had turned the gas burner on the stove on and I could barely see the flame from where I stood.  I must have been pretty small because I had to look up to see the burners.  My brother had a fork in his hand, and he put the fork in the flame to make it really hot.  I also remember he had to reach up to put the fork in the flame, so he must have been pretty little, also.  I watched in total amazement as he carefully heated the fork.  I had never seen anyone holding an eating fork in a flame of fire before!  Then in one swift movement, he grabbed my little, skinny arm and pressed the fork onto the skin right at the bend of my elbow.  In other words, he branded me.  I remember letting out a blood-curdling scream and that is where the memory ends.  Can you imagine what happened next?  I'm sure someone ran to my side only to find a fresh brand of a fork on my arm.  The four prongs of the fork remained on my arm and can even be seen today---see?  Of course, they are really faded now and have spread but can you see?"

Brandon leaned over and took her left arm in his hands to get a closer look.  Sure enough, Brandon could make out the scar faintly.

"This is unbelievable!" Brandon said halfway laughing but halfway feeling very sorry for Marilyn.  "You poor little thing.  Is that why you're so tough today?"  Brandon said pulling her close to him.  "Well, you don't have to be tough anymore.  I'll protect you and keep these things from happening to you."  He hugged her gently.

127

"OK, since I've gotten pity from you on that one, let me tell you what else he used to do to me."

"Uh-oh---can I take it?" Brandon asked looking out of the corner of his eye.

"Sure," Marilyn continued." I always wanted to tag along with my brother---I told you that. He usually didn't want me tagging along so he would take off my shoes and would leave me standing in the middle of a sticker patch. I remember standing there crying and not moving one inch. He had me believe that if I moved one step, I'd step right into a bunch of stickers. Of course, I probably could have inched my way out, but I never remember trying. I guess I cried until someone came to my rescue! I just remember standing there crying. What a baby I was!"

"Is that why you became a tomboy?" Brandon asked. "I think all of that toughened you up! So, what happened-----you don't seem like a tomboy now---not at all!"

"Oh, I don't know. I just loved running and jumping and doing those tomboy things. I never played with baby dolls, either. Mom said that when I was very young, she bought me a baby doll thinking that's what all little girls love. To her disappointment, I didn't pay any attention at all to the beautiful baby doll. Mom said I put the doll down and then started playing with the trucks my brother got. You know what I loved and was interested in the most?" Marilyn said with eyebrows lifted.

"I can't imagine. You tell me," Brandon said.

"I loved playing with horses---you know, the toy type. I'd imagine they were real. I was in heaven if I had a toy horse to play with. Once my mother bought me a rather large, white, toy horse. I remember holding it against the window sill of the car so everyone could see it. I was so proud of that horse. I think it was about nine inches tall so that was huge compared to the others I had."

"So, you really loved horses?" Brandon asked.

"Oh, yes! And I always wanted a real one. A friend of mine, Debbie, had several *real* horses. She lived on the edge of town. I always thought she was so lucky to have real horses. But she was a really good rider. She entered barrel racing competitions at the local rodeos---and she won! I could never do that, but I really admired her for her talent. I felt lucky just to get to ride with her."

"Would you like to have a real horse now?" Brandon asked.

"Oh, yes! But, to be realistic, I can't take care of a horse while I'm still in school. Maybe I could get one someday. I think they're such beautiful animals. I watched Roy Rogers and Dale Evans on television as a child and their horses were magnificent! Trigger and Buttermilk, I believe."

The rest of the morning flew by. Soon it was time to think about lunch. Brandon asked, "Rosebud, are you hungry? It's already 1:00. I didn't realize it was so late."

"Yes, I am a little hungry, but it's so wonderful here and it's so beautiful. I don't really want to leave this paradise. I know a growing boy like you really must eat something, so I'm more than happy to go with you and perhaps eat a bite."

"So, you'd rather stay here longer?" he asked with a trick up his sleeve.

"Oh, I just love being here with you and we are all alone. I'm selfish and I hate sharing you--- even for the whole 60 seconds it takes for the waitress to take our order."

"Well, I think I can do something about that," Brandon said as he turned to walk to the car. "You stay here and I'll be right back!" Brandon walked the short distance to the car. Marilyn watched every step that he took. He was the most attractive man she had ever seen. She wondered many times how she could be so lucky to meet such a wonderful man. He was such a good Samaritan, too. The townspeople loved him and he constantly helped others in need. Marilyn had already heard all about his acts of kindness from her Aunt Linda. Brandon was also successful and happy in his chosen career. He drank very little, only a glass of wine occasionally, and was careful to eat healthfully. He exercised and enjoyed physical activities.  Marilyn wouldn't change anything about him.

When Brandon reached the car, he opened the trunk and pulled out a large basket.

Marilyn squealed when she saw the basket.  She didn't know what was in it, but she really didn't care.  All she knew was that they were going to be able to stay at the park longer.  She also loved picnics of all types.  How romantic!

The basket contained two bottles of the best wine that Brandon could find and that he knew would suit Marilyn's taste.  She liked wine if it were fairly sweet and not too dry.  He also had several different kinds of fruit----strawberries, cherries, apples, and grapes.  He bought mild cheddar cheese, mozzarella cheese, and some Brie.  He knew that Brie was her very favorite type of cheese.  A box of crackers helped complete the lunch.  Of course, he added napkins, a small salt shaker and some paper plates. They both ate until they could eat no more and then lay down to relax.  A gentle breeze was blowing through the trees and it felt slightly cool.  They had time to talk about everything they wanted to talk about.  Brandon started the serious conversation.

"Sweetheart, you know that I love you more than anything else in the world, don't you?"

"Yes, because I love you that much, too."

"We have the same likes and dislikes, the same goals and the same ambitions."

"You're right about that."

"I know it's going to be hard to be apart, but I promised your parents that I wouldn't stand in the way of your getting your degree. If I acted on just my desires alone, I'd take you home with me today and you could just forget about school. Unfortunately, we can't do that."

"I know, Brandon, I know. I promised my parents also. As long as I know you're there for me, I can make it through anything. We just have to try to make it for the next nine months. Then I'll be back for the summer again, and we can spend every day together.

"If I can't go a week without seeing you, how do you think I'm going to make it for several weeks? Brandon was dead serious.

The two of them lay on their backs and looked toward the sky. Soft, fluffy, white clouds slowly floated across the baby-blue sky. Occasionally, a large bird flew by, and they even saw a butterfly or two. They wanted the day to last forever. As the sun started sinking in the western sky, they knew their hours together were fleeing. The sky turned from blue to gray, and then the setting sun turned the horizon golden.

"Guess we better pack up, sweetie," Brandon forced himself to say. He knew she didn't want the day to end, either. He had a four-hour drive back to Slaton. He was also going to help usher at the church Sunday morning, so he would have to be there earlier than usual. If they left now, they could have dinner together and then he would head for home.

They packed up the empty bottles and trash they had accumulated. They placed the basket, the pillow, and grandmother's blanket in the trunk. As Marilyn helped Brandon fold the large blanket into a smaller square, Brandon put his arms around her and kissed her affectionately. "Thank you for such a perfect picnic," he said to Marilyn who was still floating from the kiss.

"You're thanking me?" she asked. "You did everything. It was a complete surprise, and I loved every minute of it. I didn't know you were such a good picnic maker. Is there such a word as picnic maker?"

"If you say there is---there is," Brandon answered.

They drove through the park and then headed back to the campus. It was about 6:00 in the evening by this time, so they decided to get a hamburger at the campus burger house. Joe's Burgers were the best ever. They shared an order of fries, and then each had a chocolate shake. The place was packed with college kids, but the couple didn't notice anyone. They were in a world of their own. They didn't see anything around them. They didn't hear anything around them. Brandon was determined to make the dinner at the hamburger house one filled with laughter. He accomplished his mission. Marilyn laughed so hard at some of the things he told her that tears streamed down her face. She couldn't stop laughing. Brandon was pleased. Others were envious.

Marilyn kept talking. She could sense as they finished their hamburgers and fries that the time was shortly approaching when Brandon would have to drive back to Slaton. She wanted to postpone it as long as possible, but at the same time she realized Brandon had a long drive ahead of him.

"It's almost 8:00, Rosebud. We better get you back to your dorm, so I can head home."

"No, I think you just got here, Brandon. I think you were going to spend the day with me, and it is only 8:00 in the morning. We still have the whole day together. Are you confused?" Marilyn said playfully.

"Actually, yes, I *am* confused---very confused. I've been confused since the first day I met you. You have somehow gotten into my head, and I'm confused all the time. I can't think of anything else but you. I try to do my work, and I stop because I'm thinking of you. I go to the store, and I forget why I went because I'm thinking of you. I go to church and try to listen to the reverend, but I start thinking about you. I try to sleep at night, but I can't because I'm thinking of you. When I do fall asleep, I dream about you." Brandon looked deeply into her eyes. She smiled softly. "OK— let's go." Brandon knew they had to leave.

They stood up, and Brandon helped her to the car. He opened her car door, held her hand as he helped her in, and then kissed her on the cheek before he closed the door. It was only two blocks back to her dorm. Sadness was suddenly taking over their time together.

Brandon walked her to the foyer in her dormitory. Actually, the doors locked at 8:30 every night, so they got there just in time. She could have gotten in, but she would have had to get the dorm mother to unlock the front door. They didn't want to disturb her again.

Brandon held Marilyn in his arms for as long as he thought was acceptable. "I love you," he told her whispering close to her ear.

"I love you, too. Please be careful on the way home," Marilyn responded with tears swelling in her eyes. "I'll write."

With that, Brandon turned around and headed back to his car. The drive home was going to be very, *very* long.

*Dearest Brandon,*

*It's been exactly 17 minutes since I last saw you. That's already too long. Since I could think of nothing but you after you left, I decided to take a bath and then do my reading assignments in bed. I'll be singing in church early in the morning, so I really must try to get some sleep. I'll try to go to sleep now, so I can dream about you.*

*Sunday—I was right. I dreamed about you last night. In the dream, we went on another picnic together. This time, I supplied the food, and we were in the park at home. I dreamed we saw your elusive goldfish. It looked at us, too. I could see its eyes from where we stood on the bank.*

*I sang in the church choir this morning. I think I had more spirit in my voice since I had just seen you the day before. You have a wonderful, positive effect on me. After church, I grabbed a bite to eat with Carrie---of course, I had to give her another blow-by-blow reporting of our day together. She really is a special friend.*

*Good news—I have part of the second week of October free. I can leave on Thursday afternoon after my last class and can stay until Sunday afternoon. Mom will want me to start back by noon, but maybe we can push it to 1:00 pm. I hope you are free that weekend. I counted 25 days until I get home. I'll be anxiously awaiting that day.*

> *I love you,*
> *Marilyn*

Chapter Four
Home for the Weekend
October 1922


When Brandon got the letter, he immediately marked off the weekend Marilyn wrote him about. He wouldn't miss that weekend for any reason. In fact, some of his friends talked about going hiking sometime that month, but Brandon instantly decided that if the trip fell on that weekend, he would not go. No way. He liked his friends, but he loved Marilyn. He didn't know how he could go 25 days until he could be with her again. Somehow, he would make it work. He really didn't have a choice.

Marilyn and Brandon continued to write to each other many more times over the next three weeks. Then the day finally arrived for Marilyn to drive home. She packed her car prior to class, so she wouldn't miss one minute before leaving.

Brandon knew that Marilyn would be leaving the campus around 1:00 pm. According to his calculation, she should arrive sometime around 5:00 pm. He drove to the Davis home and knocked on the door.

"Hello, Brandon," Mrs. Davis said with a smile as she opened the door.

"I'm sorry Mrs. Davis, but I figured Marilyn would be driving in any minute now, and I wanted to be here when she gets in, if that is OK with you," Brandon said as politely as he could.

"I'd be disappointed in you if you didn't want to be here," she replied.

Brandon thought perhaps he would have time to talk to Mrs. Davis, since they never had a chance to talk very much.

"Before Marilyn gets here, I must tell you that I want to spend as much time with her as I possibly can. Since I know you want to spend time with her, too, maybe we could all do some things together."

"Yes, her father and I would love that, Brandon. I don't know what the two of you have planned, but why don't we go to church together Sunday morning?"

"I'd like that very much," Brandon answered.

"Then we could go to lunch together and then Marilyn should really head back after that. I don't want her to get back to the college too late."

Just as Brandon sat down to wait for Marilyn, he saw her car pulling into the driveway.

"There she is!" he announced and sprinted to the front door. Mrs. Davis had to laugh inside. She had never seen a man so smitten. *Yes*, she thought. *He was in love, too.*

Brandon ran around to her side of the car and

opened the door. Marilyn jumped out and threw her arms around him.

"OK, kids. Come in, and let's all have a tall glass of tea." Mrs. Davis said from the porch. Marilyn ran up and gave her mother a hug.

"I've missed you, Mom," Marilyn said.

The three went inside and were shortly joined by Mr. Davis. He managed to get away from the office early, knowing Marilyn was coming in.

The four of them sat at the kitchen table talking and laughing. Marilyn told them how Brandon visited her a few days after she left home and surprised her with a picnic at the park near the campus.

"Brandon has agreed to join us at church Sunday morning and then for lunch before you leave. We can get our running around done tomorrow while he is at work and then the rest of the time is yours!" Mrs. Davis said.

"I was afraid her mom was going to book the whole weekend," her father said rather sarcastically. "You two need some time to yourselves."

Brandon and Marilyn were both very appreciative of his insight. They would love to be alone together as much as possible.

"There's a dance at our old stomping grounds tomorrow night," said Brandon knowing how much Marilyn loved to dance. "Do ya want to go?"

"Oh, I was hoping we could go to a dance this weekend!" Marilyn exclaimed.

"Mr. and Mrs. Davis, why don't you join us?" Brandon asked politely. "How long has it been since the two of you have been dancing?"

"Oh, my!" Mrs. Davis giggled. "I can't even remember when. It might be fun to just watch. What do you think, Albert?" She turned to her husband to get his opinion of the offer.

"Sure! I think it's like riding a bicycle, isn't it? I think it comes back if ya give it a try," he responded.

They all laughed. Marilyn and Brandon were actually excited that her parents were going to go with them to the dance. They looked forward to Friday night.

After Brandon brought Marilyn's bags in from the car, he headed home to shower and change clothes. They decided that they would walk to the park being sure to stop to look for the fish and then drive over to the Remington home to have dinner with his parents. Marilyn was a little nervous about meeting his parents.

As they walked to the park, Marilyn reminded Brandon that they saw the giant goldfish in her dream. Maybe this would be the day! It really didn't matter if they did or not. They just wanted to be together---fish or no fish. As they walked around the pond, they saw two children staring at the water and pointing excitedly. Brandon and Marilyn joined them and saw what they were looking at. It was a large, orange fish approximately eighteen inches long. It was so close to the edge of the pond that everyone could see its eyes. Just like in Marilyn's dream! Then as soon as it appeared, it flipped its tail and then was gone in the dark-green, mossy water. How lucky they were to see it!

"This is a special day for you, Rosebud," Brandon said. "You've just seen a fish that you've never seen before and in about twenty minutes, you're going to meet my parents and you've never seen them before, either!"

"I can't wait!" Marilyn said kind of nervously.

"You're going to be fine, and they're going to love you---you'll see. Unfortunately, or maybe it is fortunately, you are going to miss meeting my sister because she is out of town. You'll meet her soon," Brandon laughed. Marilyn didn't really know what he meant by that comment, but she figured out she would know someday soon. She didn't ask.

2

Marilyn freshened up a bit when they got back to her house. She wanted to look just right, especially since this was the first time to meet Brandon's parents. She chose a pretty, pink sweater and a long, off-white skirt. She pulled a pretty hat down over her wavy, blonde hair. The evening was very cool, so she needed a light wrap. She made sure that her lipstick matched her sweater perfectly--- soft, cotton-candy pink.

"Come in—come in ---come in," Mrs. Remington said as Brandon helped Marilyn through the front door. "We've been so anxious to meet you." Mr. Remington walked up at the same time and gave Marilyn a hug.

"I've been anxious to meet you, too. Anyone who has a son who is so much fun must be pretty spectacular also!",

"You mean he's been nice and sweet and mannerly with you? Mrs. Remington added faking surprise.

"Well, I'm trying to keep him in line. It's a pretty big job," Marilyn answered. "But, someone has to do it!" Everyone laughed heartily.

Brandon's mother, Suzanne Remington, was a striking woman. She was tall and thin and very attractive. She managed to keep her hair perfectly coiffed and maintained a beautiful manicure even though she enjoyed working in her garden on a daily basis. She was very active socially and enjoyed attending several ladies' clubs around town. Suzanne was known for her kind and generous manner.

Brandon's father, Joseph, was also a striking man. Although some gray hair had crept into his dark hair over the past couple of years, he maintained his healthy shape by walking and working out. He worked his way up as a CPA in an accounting firm before branching out to open an office of his own. He enjoyed his work, but always made sure there was a healthy balance between family, work, and church. Mr. Remington was thrilled when Brandon decided to follow in his footsteps. Having a son in the family business couldn't be better. And to have a son like Brandon in the family business was perfect. What a proud father! Joseph saw it as a blessing from God to have his son working with him on a daily basis.

The evening at the Remington's went perfectly. Marilyn relaxed after getting to know the Remingtons and she felt right at home with them. Brandon's mother cooked a wonderful meal and dinner conversation was filled with laughter. After dessert, the four retired to the living room where they continued their conversation over after-dinner drinks for the Remingtons and raspberry tea for Marilyn. She never drank hard alcohol, and always preferred tea or soft drinks, or perhaps just a little sweet wine.

After many more laughs, Mr. and Mrs. Remington decided to let Brandon and Marilyn have some time to themselves; after all, they had to spend so much time away from each other.

"Good night, Marilyn. It was such a

143

pleasure meeting you. Please come visit us again soon," Mrs. Remington said sincerely. Mr. Remington nodded in agreement with a smile.

As soon as Brandon's parents retired to their bedroom, Brandon pulled Marilyn into his arms and held her tightly. "You were wonderful tonight, Rosebud. Just like you always are. My parents love you---I can tell." Brandon then kissed Marilyn, a longer kiss than usual, with more feeling, if that were even possible. They walked out onto the front porch.

Neither said a word for almost two minutes; they just held each other and looked at the stars. The darkness was so beautiful. The sky was dark velvet, dotted with tiny diamonds sparkling against it. Then Brandon said, "I guess I'd better take you home. Your parents will be waiting." Brandon didn't want to take her home, but that meant he'd also get to kiss her goodnight again. And he did.

3

Friday morning began as most days do around the Davis household. Mrs. Davis got up to fix breakfast for her husband before he left for the law office. Marilyn sipped on her orange juice while she gave them the rundown of the night before. After breakfast, mother and daughter were on a mission to check out the "Going Out of Business" sale at the Browning Furniture Company. Mrs. Davis was interested in buying a new sofa and wanted Marilyn's opinion on which one to buy.

The Davis women met Aunt Linda for lunch again on Friday. Aunt Linda had already heard that her matchmaking was 20-20 for Brandon and Marilyn, but she wanted to hear some of the stories firsthand. In fact, she reserved the same table at Maudie's. Lunch was so much fun!

Marilyn told Aunt Linda all about going to the fundraiser with Mark even though she really wanted to be with Brandon----and then how Brandon saw her picture in the paper---and saw Mark's mother in their car--but that Brandon seemed to handle it all in style. Then Marilyn told her the story about the picnic and what fun they had. Aunt Linda hung on every word. She loved every minute of every story.

Marilyn was anxious to get home to make sure she had just the right dress for the dance that night. Brandon and Marilyn loved to dance and having her parents with them was a special bonus. There was no telling what was going to happen!

Brandon arrived at Marilyn's house right on time. He had washed the car and made sure the inside was spotless. He walked Marilyn out to the car, opened her door for her and at the same time, helped open the door for her mother. *Such a gentleman*, Mrs. Davis thought to herself.

Brandon told a few jokes on the way to the dance and had everyone in stitches.

*"OK, there was a very important businessman who was running a little late to a very*

*important business meeting. He drove around and around and couldn't find a place to park his car. It was a very important meeting, and he just couldn't be late! Fearing he'd be late to the meeting, the man prayed to God: "Lord, please help me find a parking place. If you do, I'll go to church every Sunday morning for the rest of my life! And I'll tithe ten percent of what I make!" Just when the words got out of his mouth, a car pulled out of a space right in front of him. "Never mind," the man said, "I've found one!"* Everyone in the car roared at Brandon's joke.

"No, wait! I have another one," Brandon said excitedly. Everyone was waiting in anticipation of his next joke. "Here goes---*A man was driving around town in a pick-up full of pink flamingos. A policeman pulled the pick-up over and asked the man what he was doing with a truck full of flamingos. When the driver didn't give the officer a satisfactory answer, the officer told him to take the flamingos to the zoo. "I'll do that," the driver said and off he went. The next day, the same officer spotted the man again with the same pick-up full of pink flamingos, but this time they were all wearing sunglasses. "What are you doing?" the officer asked the man. "I thought I told you to take these flamingos to the zoo!" "I did," the man answered. "They enjoyed themselves so much at the zoo that I thought I'd take them to the beach today."*

Mr. and Mrs. Remington chuckled until their sides hurt. Marilyn had tears running down her cheeks. Brandon just smiled. He really loved making people laugh.

"Ok, ok, ok!" Brandon added among the laughter. "I have one more joke, but this is the last one. Any more and I'll have to start charging!"

"OK—here it goes. *A man brought a friend home for dinner unexpectedly. When he told his wife she said, "Are you crazy? I am not dressed--- curlers are in my hair---I have not put on any make- up---the house is a wreck----I haven't been to the grocery store, and there is no food!! Why in the world did you ask him to dinner?" "Well," he answered calmly. "Because he told me he was thinking about getting married."*

"Maybe we should skip the dance and just drive around," Mrs. Davis said giggling.

"No," Brandon responded, "You're not getting out of it this easy."

The Davises had so much fun on the way to the dance, but they were anxious to see Brandon and Marilyn dancing together. They had no idea what would be in store for them!

They arrived at the dance and walked in. There seemed to be plenty of people there, and it was a little difficult finding an empty table. When the music started, the Davises decided to be observers. After all, it had been many years since they had been to a dance. They really didn't know if times had passed them by. They would probably know the older dances but the newer ones? They wouldn't know any of the newer dances, so they chose to just watch and make mental notes.

Brandon and Marilyn tore up the dance floor. From slow to medium to fast, no dance left them motionless. They danced every song. With a little encouragement from the young couple, Mr. and Mrs. Davis took to the dance floor. Marilyn danced with her father, and Brandon danced with her mother. All it took was a little coaxing to get them started, and then they danced almost every dance. In no time at all, the Davises were dancing as good as anyone there.

"I've never seen my parents having so much fun! This is great! Look at how they're enjoying themselves! Who would've ever thought!" Marilyn told Brandon over the noise of the music. "This is one of the best things we've ever done!"

"Whew!" Mrs. Davis said to everyone when they finally sat down to catch their breaths. I haven't had that much exercise in years!"

The evening was a huge success. They left the dance at midnight and arrived home shortly thereafter. As Brandon walked everyone to the door, Mr. Davis said, "I had a great time tonight. I probably won't be able to walk tomorrow, but I had fun tonight! Everyone laughed. Brandon stole a quick kiss from Marilyn and then drove home. The second night with Marilyn had just ended. He would only have one more evening with her. At least he would have her all to himself on Saturday. He thoroughly enjoyed the dinner with his parents on Thursday night and being with her parents tonight, but he looked forward to monopolizing her time on Saturday, and that's just what he did.

## 4

The way that they planned the day, Marilyn would get up bright and early on Saturday morning. She wanted to have breakfast with her parents, and then get ready for Brandon to pick her up around 8:30. She was excited about going to the children's home with Brandon to distribute books. Brandon volunteered to deliver reading books to the children, and he wanted Marilyn to go with him. It was just one of the many community services that he did each year.

After that, they were going to go to the county fair. The fair came to the county seat of Clarkstown every October, and most of the people from the surrounding towns attended. Brandon had been going with his family since he was too little to remember. Now, being the young 'community volunteer type' that he had become, Brandon had been chosen to be one of the judges in the art contest. Judging would take place on Saturday for the awards to be announced that evening. Brandon didn't feel that he knew that much about art, but he was willing to give it a try. He didn't know what category he would be judging until he arrived, but he wasn't worried. He figured he could tell a good painting if he saw one. Besides, he would have Marilyn along, and maybe she could be his assistant.

Brandon figured that after his judging job ended, they would have time to see the sights for themselves. Marilyn loved animals, so a cruise through the animal barns was going to be top of the list of activities. Brandon loved to eat, so they planned on having at least one corndog, one stick of cotton candy, one caramel apple, and a turkey leg. That sounded like a well-balanced meal to them!

The rides were going to be a different matter. Brandon loved riding the scarier rides---like the giant roller coaster and the giant Ferris wheel. Marilyn leaned more to the merry-go-round and the bumper cars. To make the evening interesting, Marilyn agreed to try anything. Maybe, she thought, Brandon would have to hold her tightly for her safety. She liked that idea. OK, that was the plan.

When Brandon and Marilyn planned the day, they figured they would return home at least by midnight. It would be a full day of activities, and they would be together the entire time.

Brandon picked Marilyn up right at 9:30 as he had promised, and they drove fifteen minutes to the Buckner Children's Home on the outside of town. Marilyn noticed boxes of books in the back seat of his car and inquired about the procedure.

"Brandon, how do you know what books go to what age child?"

"I wouldn't know, but my secretary's

daughter is an elementary school teacher so she helped me with it. See these stickers in the right-hand corner? Age range," he said with confidence. "Now all we have to do is ask their age and hand them a book. There is some high-level decision making that will be required of you, however," he said seriously.

"There is? What is it?" Marilyn answered. She should know by now that Brandon is a jokester, and he was probably leading her into something.

"Well, if you see a book with trucks and cars on it, you should probably give it to a boy. If it has ballerinas or dolls on the cover, hand it to a girl. Animals can go either way. I hope you don't make a mistake and embarrass me," he said starting to laugh.

"I think I can handle that. If I get confused, I'll pass it on to you," Marilyn responded jokingly.

Passing out the books went really well. The children were so excited, and it made Marilyn and Brandon feel so good inside to be doing it. "You know," said Brandon, "there are so many small things that people can do for others, but they don't even think about it. Giving to others is so rewarding, and most people miss out on it. See how good you feel just giving books to these children? Giving to others is more of a gift to the giver than to the receiver. Why don't more people see that?" Brandon was rarely dead serious, but Marilyn saw that he really meant every word he said.

"I knew a woman who did something really special at Christmas. I think her name was Margaret. Instead of giving expensive gifts to her family when they didn't need or want for anything, she went to the clothing store and toy store, bought shopping carts full of items, then drove to the poor part of town to give everything away to the children there. She felt so good doing it the first time that it became a yearly activity for her. What's more important---- an expensive sweater given to someone who already probably has ten of them, or shopping carts full of clothes and toys for the poor children who only have one pair of pants and a few handmade toys? Why don't more people see this, Marilyn?"

"I honestly don't think people even think about it. Let's set an example and see it if spreads!" Marilyn offered. She was so proud of Brandon and got another insight into what kind of person he really was. Every day she loved him more and more.

They arrived at the fairgrounds around 11:00 am. Clarkstown was about thirty minutes away, so Marilyn and Brandon had plenty of time to discuss things. For the first time, Marilyn began thinking about how she could give back to her community. She had never thought about it, either. Of course, she had volunteered to do various community, fund-raisers and volunteered her time on community service, but she wanted to do something where she would give of herself, not just her time, but her resources. People get busy and so wrapped up in their own achievements that they forget about one

152

of the best opportunities in the world---and it is right under their noses.

Brandon found the Creative Arts Building and reported to duty right on time. Opening his assignment envelope, he read that his assignment was to judge 'portraits' and 'photography.' Looking at Marilyn he said, "I don't really know anything about portrait drawing, but I can tell if the drawing looks like the photograph the artist used. And photography? Well, I'll just have to give it my best shot."

"You'll do fine. You can tell a good picture when you see one," Marilyn said encouragingly. "It's like when you saw my picture in the paper with Mark. You thought that was a pretty good picture, didn't you?" Smiling widely, she knew she got to him with that statement. He grabbed her around the throat pretending he was going to choke her. Then he stole a quick kiss.

"Did you have to bring that up and ruin a perfectly good day?" Brandon questioned with a serious look on his face. Marilyn giggled. She loved him so much.

The fact of the matter was that Brandon couldn't tell a good picture when he saw one and solely depended on clues from Marilyn who walked with him but across the table from where he was. Brandon kept glancing up as he viewed each picture. If Marilyn smiled, he was on target. If she ignored him, he would pass on to the next picture. If she looked at his eyes, that picture was going to get a ribbon!  Easy, Brandon thought, as long as he had Marilyn as his assistant! Judging was a huge success!  Upon a choosing the winners, the art director acknowledged agreement with the selections.

"I don't know what I would have done without you!" he said hugging Marilyn as they walked out of the building. "Really---what would I have done!  These people were depending on me to do good job, and I didn't want to let them down! Thanks so much!"

Marilyn was proud that she could help him out in his judging assignment.  Now all the duties were fulfilled, and they would have the rest of the day to themselves!

"OK, let's be organized about this," Brandon commented seriously. "Eat, then ride, then look.  Then we'll repeat it---eat, then ride, then look." Marilyn started laughing as she repeated, "Eat---ride---look."

"Whatever you say, judge," she answered. Brandon took the opportunity to hug Marilyn, and then he kissed her cheek.  He knew he had to control himself.  Don't kiss her on the lips--- because then he couldn't think of anything else for the rest of the day.

They didn't follow the eat-ride-look routine, but they managed to eat everything they originally talked about, and they rode almost every ride in the park.  Marilyn even survived the roller coaster.

When she wasn't screaming, she was laughing. Brandon got as much a kick out of watching her as he did with the ride. This ride gave Brandon plenty of chances to hold Marilyn close. She may have screamed a few extra times just so he would hold her closer. "Hold me, Brandon! Hold me so I don't fall out! Hold me tighter Brandon! I'm afraid---I'm afraid!!"

"Marilyn, the ride is over---it has stopped---get a grip." Brandon tried to seem as nonchalant as possible, but the biggest smile crept across his face.

Between the rides and eating, the couple had so much fun just walking down the midway. The sky was dark, but there were sparkling lights everywhere. Everything was so colorful and the musical sounds floated through the air. Laughter and screams were rampant. Brandon and Marilyn held hands as they walked through the crowd. Sometimes his arm was around her waist. Marilyn never wanted the night to end. They left a little while before the fair closed, since they had a thirty-minute drive back home. Brandon wanted to get Marilyn home before midnight.

When Brandon walked Marilyn to the door, he stopped before opening the door.

"Marilyn, I had a great time today, but the more I'm with you, the more I want to be with you. I know you are leaving tomorrow, and I am already dreading it. It's not getting any easier."

"I know Brandon-- I know." Marilyn

responded in a depressed tone. "I feel the same way. Leaving you will be one of the hardest things I'll have to do."

Brandon held her face in his hands and kissed her for a long time. It was the most affectionate kiss Brandon had ever given her. With this kiss, Brandon tried to tell her how much he loved her. Neither said a word. Marilyn walked in the house, and Brandon walked back to his car.

They were going to church the following morning with Marilyn's parents and then to lunch following the service. Marilyn had a surprise planned for Brandon. She was going to sing a beautiful religious solo, and Brandon didn't even know about it. Actually, it was a surprise to Marilyn that the choir director asked her to sing, but she was happy to do it. Brandon had never heard Marilyn sing before. He knew she was a music major in college, but singing had never been mentioned. Marilyn's parents knew she would be singing, but Brandon didn't. What a beautiful surprise was waiting for him!

5

Brandon drove to the Davis house to drive Marilyn and her parents to church.

"Good morning, Brandon!" Mrs. Davis said as she answered the door. "I hear you and Marilyn had a great time last night at the fair! I can't wait to hear all about it."

"Yes, we did! We had so much…" Brandon stopped when Marilyn entered the room. He was overtaken by her beauty. Marilyn looked striking in her long, navy-blue dress with a white lace collar. A sash tied around her middle accentuated her thin waist. Brandon was speechless. Then realizing he looked and sounded ridiculous, he continued, "We had so much fun."

"Yes, we did!" Marilyn said cheerfully. "We'll tell you all about it at lunch," she said looking at her parents.

They left the house, drove to the church, and walked up to one of the front pews. The Davises always sat near the front, but it was particularly important today since Marilyn was going to sing. Brandon still did not know anything about it.

The service was very nice. The sermon was meaningful. After the prayer, Marilyn rose from the pew, walked to the front, and stood near the organ. Brandon looked over at Mrs. Davis with an inquisitive look. She gave him a small wink and a grin.

The music started and after a few introductory notes, Marilyn began singing. Her voice resonated throughout the sanctuary. It was the most beautiful voice Brandon had ever heard. He never dreamed she could sing so well. He was so proud of her and couldn't wait to tell her. At the end of the hymn, Marilyn returned to her seat next to Brandon. Once seated, she turned her eyes up to meet his. She had a slight grin on her face. She wanted to surprise him, and she certainly did.  He smiled back and took her hand.  Her parents smiled at her and nodded proudly. Brandon was on top of the world. He was madly in love with a beautiful girl, and now he finds out that she can sing like an angel!

Several people approached Marilyn after the service to compliment her on her wonderful musical contribution.  She thanked them politely and shook their hands.

Everyone walked back to the car.  "What a wonderful surprise!" Brandon said, "I get the feeling I was the only one who didn't know.  Every time I think I know Marilyn, she does some other marvelous thing!  I've never heard a voice so beautiful!"

"Yes, she's pretty special," her father said hugging his daughter.  Brandon wanted to hug her, too, but thought he had better wait.

At the restaurant, Marilyn and Brandon had a chance to tell her parents all about the night at the fair.  "This brings back memories of the old days when we used to go to the fair." Mr. Davis said looking at his wife and smiling.  They, too, had been to the fair on many occasions and remembered the good times they had.

The funniest story Brandon told was about the art judging assignment.  Brandon told how he didn't know what pictures to choose and how Marilyn helped him from across the table.  They all started laughing so hard they couldn't talk.  The Davis's understood why they always heard the couple laughing. Brandon had such a sense of humor. It was the way he phrased things. He just had a special way of bringing out the humor in any situation.

"Oh! We really must be going!" Mrs. Davis said as she glanced at her watch. "The time has gotten away from us. We were just enjoying ourselves so much---thanks to you, Brandon."

Saying it was time to go was like issuing a death sentence to Brandon. He knew Marilyn had to leave to go back to the campus. It made him ill. Back at the house, Brandon helped Marilyn with her bags. Her parents hugged her good-bye and then went inside the house. They wanted to give the couple some privacy before Marilyn left. Brandon was upset but held it together until he looked at Marilyn. Tears were slowing filling her eyes. With that, Brandon grabbed Marilyn, hugged her like he had never before and then kissed her. It was a rather bold move considering her parents were probably looking out the windows. Brandon cared, but he didn't care.

It had begun sprinkling with an imminent promise of rain so Brandon helped her into the car and then waved good-bye. Brandon reached down, picked another wildflower and held it up as if to say, "See, another floral shop right here next to your driveway." They both grinned. It was a good way to end their visit together----with humor instead of tears.

Chapter Five
The Relationship Grows
November 1932

They had already counted the days. It would be exactly 36 days before Marilyn would be back for Thanksgiving. Brandon wasn't going to allow that. He could possibly handle fifteen days at the most. He would figure out a way to see Marilyn sooner than that.

As it turned out, Marilyn's calendar for November was packed with musical performances and recitals. Brandon and her parents drove down to catch one of her shows but drove back that evening after the performance. Brandon really didn't have any time to be alone with her but just seeing her made him feel exhilarated.

"Brandon?" Marilyn asked inquisitively. "There is one weekend that I have a break. If I drive home, we could spend most of the weekend together. I've been dying to go dancing with you again." They agreed that she would drive in on Friday afternoon, and they would go dancing on Saturday. It's one thing to sing and dance in the university musicals; it's quite another thing to dance with someone you love--- laughing and singing along with the music. And, then it is quite a different thing to slow dance and hold your love tightly in your arms, swaying to the beautiful sounds of the music and losing yourself in the feeling. Marilyn loved dancing so much she would go dancing every night if she could.

They exchanged several letters over the next couple of weeks, telling each other the activities that were keeping them busy from day to day. The Friday finally arrived when Marilyn could drive home to be with Brandon. She wasn't able to leave quite as early as she did last time, but she'd arrive in time to have dinner with him. He was waiting for her, of course, and she knew he would be.

Jumping out of her car, Marilyn hugged Brandon as he spun her around, her feet flying off the ground. She squealed excitedly. Of course, they were both laughing.

"Oh! It's been so long since I've seen you---almost a year!" Brandon said trying to sound serious.

"Well, I saw someone who looked like you just a couple of weeks ago. Was that not you?" Marilyn asked, going along with the playfulness.

"I don't think it was me," Brandon answered. "It feels more like a year since I've seen you. I hope you're not two-timing me with someone else!"

Marilyn's parents walked out on the front porch to greet her and take her bags.

"Unless y'all have another place in mind, Aunt Linda wants you to join her at the Stoneleigh Restaurant tonight," Mrs. Davis mentioned. "She really wants to see the two of you!"

Brandon was a little disappointed at first, but he didn't let it show; he wanted Marilyn all to himself---all to himself and alone. Marilyn felt the same way but responded, "I guess it's the least we can do---after all, she's the one who introduced us!"

What they didn't know was that Aunt Linda had something special up her sleeve. It was going to be a surprise for both of them.

Marilyn ran in to freshen up after her drive. In just a few minutes, she was ready to go.

At the restaurant, they were greeted by the maître d' who escorted them down a hallway to the back of the restaurant. Aunt Linda was waiting for them.

"Darlings!" she said when she saw them. "I would absolutely love to have dinner with two of my favorite people in the whole world. We would laugh and tell stories like never before! We would have an absolute marvelous time. But---if I were you, I'd want to be alone together. Your time alone is limited. So, I've planned a very special dinner for the two of you. It's all been paid for, and you can stay here as long as you like." She then led them into their own private dining room.

Brandon had heard this restaurant had special rooms for private dining, but he had never seen them. They couldn't believe their luck. Good ol' Aunt Linda. They decided they really owed her this time.

The room was small with a table for just two people. The chairs were a peacock design; the backs were tall and curved slightly inward on each side. When pulled up to the table, the chair backs formed a private enclosure around the couple. Directly across from them was a beautifully landscaped rock fountain with running water. The soft, trickling sound of the water was relaxing and added a melodic backdrop to their conversation. Real tropical plants with beautiful flowers surrounded them. The scent of the trickling water and the flowering greenery was clean and refreshing. The room was lit with candlelight except for a few, tiny lights accenting the waterfall. It was a very private, very romantic retreat. Just what Aunt Linda ordered!

"Is this paradise, Marilyn? I think it must be. Or, am I dreaming? Are we really alone together in this beautiful place?"

"I've never seen a more beautiful place," Marilyn answered in awe. "I feel like we are in some tropical retreat---not in our little hometown in Texas. We'll pretend we are on a beautiful Hawaiian island!"

The dinner was exquisite---a five-course, gourmet meal. The service was even better. They had everything they needed with minimal interruptions. They never knew how the waiters knew it, but when a glass was empty, someone quietly stepped in to fill it.

"So far," Brandon said, "Our life together

has been one surprise after another."

"I hope the surprises never end if they are like this one," Marilyn said.

"Or like that Sunday morning when the most gorgeous girl sang the most beautiful song in church---oh yes---that was you!" Brandon said smiling. He took her hand in his and squeezed it gently. Pulling her closer to him, he leaned forward to give her a soft kiss. It was one of many that evening.

At the end of their lovely dining experience, Brandon and Marilyn just sat staring at each other. This was definitely a life memory for each of them. They had a wonderful time together, the food was exquisite, and the atmosphere was perfect. What a lovely, lovely evening, thanks to Aunt Linda.

Saturday was going to prove to be just as exciting and romantic. Marilyn spent the morning with her parents and then met Brandon for lunch. They went to Eblen Pharmacy to buy a special card to send to Aunt Linda. They both wanted to thank her in a special handwritten card, writing what they wanted to say straight from the heart. Marilyn told Brandon about seeing him the very first time when he stood outside on the sidewalk when she ran in to do some shopping. Marilyn had never really told him that before.

"Brandon, I saw you outside on the sidewalk. I can't explain how I felt. It was almost magical. I wanted to walk right out there and introduce myself but I'd *never* do that! Then when I saw you walk in the pharmacy, I got this funny fluttering in my stomach! You do that to me! Still do! I can't explain it.

2

Brandon had built up enough confidence with Marilyn that he was willing to introduce her to his sister, Bonnie.

Bonnie was two years younger than Brandon. She was always the 'tag along' little sister as they were growing up. She was somewhat of a tomboy and preferred playing football with her brother than doing more of the girlish things. Along with following him around, she sometimes became the guinea pig. Once, Brandon rigged a clothesline wire from the top of a tree twenty-feet high to a stake on the ground about thirty feet from the base of the tree. He placed the wire through the loose handles of a number-two washtub. From the top of the tree, the washtub slid down the wire until it reached the ground. It was supposed to resemble a ski jump or a gondola ride. Guess who was chosen to be the first passenger of the washtub? It is a miracle that the handles didn't break with the weight, or the wire didn't come loose from the tree, or the stake didn't come up out of the ground. Any number of things could have gone wrong and could have caused a disaster. Fortunately, their mother found out about the adventure before the second send off. Bonnie was saved from a second slide--- and maybe her death!

Another time, Brandon convinced Bonnie to hold on to the back of a motorized cart. With Bonnie hanging on with all her might, Brandon pushed the pedal to the floor and went as fast as the cart would go around the track. Bonnie's screams had no effect on his intention to scare her to death---if anything, it fueled it. If she had fallen off, her whole body would have been one giant, bloody mess. She survived that, also. With everything Brandon and Bonnie went through together, they formed a very strong bond with each other.

"Oh! The elusive Bonnie----I'm finally going to get to meet her?" Marilyn said jokingly.

"Yes, you are----and it is bound to be quite an experience," Brandon answered. "Come on---let's go and get this over with, so we can go dancing tonight!" Brandon was always kidding----that fact Marilyn already knew.

They drove to Brandon's house and walked through the front door. "Bonnie?" Brandon called out. "Anyone home?"

He knew his parents were gone for the afternoon, but Bonnie was supposed to be there. Bonnie came bouncing out of the kitchen. "Of course, I'm here, big brother. I wouldn't miss meeting Marilyn for anything in the world!"

A quick glance at Marilyn and Bonnie said, "You are beautiful, Marilyn---much too pretty for Brandon. Do you want me to fix you up with a really nice guy---- handsome, too?"

With that comment, Brandon grabbed Bonnie in a neck hold and pretended to be choking her. Her voice muffled by the chokehold, Bonnie managed to barely say, in a raspy voice, "He's rich, too!—*gasp*---I've been known to set up some pretty good dates. I have ---*gasp*---an especially wonderful man in mind."

Brandon released his hold and the three of them laughed until they were crying. "Do you see why I haven't introduced you to Bonnie before?" Brandon managed to get out. They all hugged and felt like family---even Marilyn felt like part of the family already.

They sat in the living room and talked for almost two hours. Brandon described in detail how Aunt Linda arranged the romantic dinner for them the night before. Marilyn told Bonnie about the picnic surprise that Brandon arranged and Brandon told about the Sunday morning singing surprise. Bonnie loved hearing about everything. She was always interested in all the details, and if it involved her brother, she wanted to know everything—everything.

Time was getting away from them, so they agreed to a quick sandwich there before heading for the dance. They didn't know it then, but the dance was going to provide another surprise for them.

Brandon drove Marilyn back to her house so she could change clothes. She picked out a really pretty dress that Brandon had never seen before. A single ruffle twirled around the hem and another ruffle bordered the neckline. Brandon also looked quite handsome in his navy-blue slacks and pale-yellow shirt. He knew his tie would come off after he started dancing and heated up. Marilyn kept him dancing every song, but he loved it, too. Marilyn was so full of life that she appeared to float across the dance floor. Her eyes sparkled with happiness and enthusiasm. Brandon could easily sit and watch Marilyn the entire night, but dancing with her was so much fun. He loved having a dancing partner who was synchronized with him perfectly. He didn't have to second guess; he knew right where she'd be for all the dips and turns.

Brandon and Marilyn had a great time dancing to all the modern tunes. Some were slow-- some were fast. As far as they were concerned, they were the only two people on the dance floor that night. Then the music stopped, and the announcer said something special was going to take place. There was going to be a couples' dance contest starting with the very next song. The announcer encouraged everyone to participate. All the couples who were brave enough to compete would start dancing when the music started. The music would change frequently, requiring a different dance style with each change. Many of the couples were seen shaking their heads, responding, "No, thank you!" to the announcer's invitation. Others just walked off the floor.

"What do ya think?" Marilyn asked Brandon with excitement in her eyes. A huge smile was on her face.

"Oh, gosh, Marilyn. I don't think I can dance that well," Brandon said knowing that they would definitely enter the contest anyway.

"Sure, you dance beautifully!"

"But I don't know which dance goes with what music! Besides, I know one fast dance and one slow dance and that is it!"

"Just let me handle that---follow me---I'll lead you into it."

"I don't know----" Brandon said hesitantly.

"Yes, you do----now get ready!" Marilyn dragged him to the *center* of the dance floor. She figured if she got him out that far, there was less chance he would walk away.

Brandon turned slightly as if heading back to the place where they had been sitting.

"No--no—no--- you're not getting off that easy!" Marilyn exclaimed.

Brandon was just acting. He knew the minute the announcer said there was going to be a competition that they would be in it. He was just playing with

Marilyn.

They joined the other contestants out on the floor. Everyone appeared nervous until the dancing started, and then one could see the competitiveness coming out. Brandon and Marilyn were having a blast, and they enjoyed every second. When the music finally stopped, the couples remained out on the floor, panting and short of breath. Sweat was beaded on their faces. Brandon hugged Marilyn as they laughed out loud.

While Brandon and Marilyn danced their hearts out, the judges saw a coordinated couple--- moves synchronized with each other perfectly. They looked like they had practiced together for years, but in reality, this was only their second time to dance together.

With everyone anxious to hear the results of the contest, the announcer stepped to the microphone. "And the winners--- the couple who will receive a $50 gift certificate---$25 each –is-----Brandon Remington and Marilyn Davis!"

Everyone cheered and clapped. The people who didn't enter the competition agreed with the judge's choice. Brandon and Marilyn didn't know there was a prize for the winning couple! What a nice surprise!

Turning to Marilyn, Brandon said, "Marilyn, you take my gift certificate also and buy anything you want."

"Great! I want to buy some toys and books for the children at the children's home. Christmas is right around the corner. What do you think?" Marilyn already knew what Brandon thought. She had been a good student of his philosophy of giving.

Saturday evening was at its end. Marilyn and Brandon had so much fun at the dance and then to win the dance contest---what a surprise! Brandon walked Marilyn to the door, held her like he never wanted to let her go, and kissed her goodnight. Neither mentioned that she would be leaving the next day. When Brandon turned to walk down the sidewalk to his car, he glanced up at the stars. They were like diamonds on a velvet-black blanket. The slight breeze felt so good against his face. It moved the tops of the trees ever so gently. He felt so thankful for his wonderful life. What could be better? *Well, having Marilyn for my wife could be better!*

4

On Sunday, they attended church together and joined her parents for a light lunch. The minutes seemed like seconds. It was time to go. Brandon walked Marilyn to her car, carrying her stuffed suitcase and carry bag.

"What in the world do you have in here, Marilyn? Bricks?" Brandon said as he faked huffing and puffing.

"No, I couldn't decide what to bring, so I

kind of overdid it!" she answered.

"I should say so!  You'd think you'd have a little pity of the poor person who has to carry these bags for you-----by the way---that would be me!"

"Oh, brother----"

"I'm not your brother, either."  Brandon was always quick on his feet.

"Who do you think carried these things to my car when I was leaving the university to get here?  Hmmm?"

"Must have been some really strong guy like me!  You know, physically fit, muscular but not too muscular…"

"Yeah, sure.  I did it ----all my little, skinny, frail, weak self!"

"Uh huh, sure."  Brandon knew she had.

Brandon waved goodbye then leaned in her car window to give her a soft kiss.  Sadness was already setting in again. They knew it would be Thanksgiving before they would be able to see each other again.

Brandon's heart sank as Marilyn's car pulled out of the driveway. Just before she pulled away from the house, she blew a kiss to Brandon. How he wanted to kiss her again!  How he wanted to hold her again! He actually thought about motioning for her to come back but then thought otherwise. *Come on, Brandon,* he thought. *Get a grip.* He watched as her car disappeared around the corner before he moved.

### Chapter Six
### Summersong Comes to Life
### January 2007

John and Diane worked constantly on the house on
Summersong Lane for almost two years before they
felt it was complete. The yard became a work of art
with seasonal color bursting out in a carefully
planned landscape design. Since it was rather cold,
Diane planted pansies along the flowerbed border.
They could stand the snow if it came.

The white, picket fence was repaired and repainted
white. The cracked and uneven sidewalk was
replaced with a cobblestone walkway filled in with
a low-growing ground cover. The front porch was
repaired and painted a light-gray color. Two large
white rocking chairs rested on the porch. Pretty
floral cushions added color and comfort. A small
wicker table stood between the chairs and was
rarely seen without a vase of fresh flowers. Since
moving in, Diane tried to keep fresh flowers in the
porch vase and also in the vase at the end of the
driveway. A brick column at the end of the drive
was actually one of a pair that held a gate for
entering the backyard. The left column, as well as
the gate, had been gone for many, many years.
John and Diane decided to keep the right column in
tact since it was built with a stone vase on the top.
Several times since they moved in, Diane noticed
that someone had placed cut flowers in the vase.
Some thoughtful neighbor, Diane surmised. Every
plank of cracked wood was replaced and then the

entire house was painted a pale, creamy-yellow--
very close to the original color as far as John could
tell. New, wood shingles covered the roof.
Window boxes, painted green as an accent, were
carefully hung under each window. They would
hold beautiful pink geraniums in the summer and
purple cabbage in the winter. A cheerful wreath
always hung on the front door and was changed out
according to seasons. Diane made sure she had a
wreath for fall, spring, summer, and, of course,
Christmas. She made them herself.

The outside of the house was picture perfect-- a
scene right out of the Better Homes and Gardens
magazine. The garden was equally pristine. Except
for the pink-rose bush that had been carefully
tended to by someone in the neighborhood, John
had to remove and then replace all the landscaping
greenery. He did a very nice job.

The inside of the house took on a similar
transformation. The end result was a beautiful, light
and airy, living environment. John and Diane were
very, very happy with the way the house looked,
inside and out.

"John," Diane said. "I think we've taken the
house back to its original condition. Do you ever
think about the people who used to live here?"
Diane asked inquisitively. "I feel like someone is
still here--- like they are looking over us. It's not a
bad feeling----just curious, I think."

"Oh, I think anyone who moves into a house
thinks about the former occupants a little. I can

imagine what this house looked like when it was brand new, and I can imagine how the people felt when they first moved in. Look how excited we were when we moved in and remember the shape it was in!!

"I just always have the feeling that there is someone in the house looking over us----in a positive way, I mean--like they care and they want us to be happy. Even when I am out in the yard, I sense someone walking with me out in the garden, and I sense someone with me when I trim the rose bushes. Funny thing---isn't it?"

2

Just when John and Diane felt that they had finished renovating their home, Diane started feeling nauseous in the mornings. She suspected that she might be pregnant, and her suspicion was confirmed when she visited Dr. Bryce's office. Although John and Diane talked many times about wanting children, it was still going to be a big surprise to John. They had been so wrapped up in the renovation, they didn't think too much about it. Diane didn't know how she was going to tell John, but she wanted it to be something special.

"John," Diane said as she walked through the living room one evening. "Which extra room should be made into a nursery someday?"

"Oh, I guess the room on the other side of the hallway. It's closer than the room down the hall, and it would be easier to hear a baby's cry,"

John answered.

"Should we go ahead and buy some baby furniture?  We'll need a bassinet, a little chest of drawers, a rocking chair, and perhaps a changing table."

"Well, why don't we go ahead and get the furniture you want for the living room and then get a bed for the guest room in case we have house guests.  We have a little time to think about baby furniture." John was always organized and systematic in his approach to any situation.

"OK, but we should probably have it in place by the first part of April," Diane said nonchalantly as she folded the clothes she had washed earlier in the day.

John looked up at Diane with a puzzled look on his face. "Are you trying to tell me something, Diane---are you?"

With a glimmer in her eye and a huge smile on her face, Diane said, "Yes---I'm pregnant!"

"Oh, my gosh! Honey!  That's wonderful!" John exclaimed.  "When?  When?"

"Dr. Durley said the baby should arrive around the middle of April---April 17 to be exact."

"OK, how about let's get the baby furniture first and THEN get the living room furniture!" John was laughing--- he was so excited.  He hugged

Diane and kissed her affectionately. "I can't think of anything better, Diane. This is just what we wanted. I'm going to be a daddy? Wow!" John responded just like Diane had hoped he would.

Diane handled her pregnancy well. She got over her morning sickness quickly and settled in to the task of furnishing the nursery. She chose a butterfly motif for the room's design. John painted butterflies as a border around the ceiling and cut out butterflies to use for a mobile over the bassinet. John and Diane enjoyed every minute they spent getting the nursery ready for their new arrival.

Little John was born on April 13, 2008 at 11:00 am. Diane had a relatively easy delivery with a very short labor. She felt extremely fortunate considering this was her first child, and she had heard horror stories of long labors and difficult deliveries. John was the perfect father, assisting Diane every chance he got with feeding and diapering the baby. Little John grew quickly and was soon toddling all through the house. He was a precious, bubbly, little boy with tasseled-blonde hair and blue eyes. He was certainly the apple of his father's eye.

3

The day was so nice outside. The weather was perfect and fluffy white clouds were playfully floating overhead. So, when Diane had a doctor's appointment, her mother came to stay with Little John. They loved sitting on a quilt, spread over the carpet of grass, and playing with some of Little

John's toys.  As they were in the backyard on the quilt, a nice, elderly lady walked down the driveway to the back where they were sitting.  Diane's mother thought she was one of the neighbors.

"Hello!" the nice lady said to Little John and his grandmother.  "Isn't he the cutest little boy you've ever seen?"

"Well, certainly!  But I'm his grandmother so, of course, I'm prejudiced!"

"I enjoy watching him so much.  He's growing up so fast, though!"

"Yes, he is!  He's getting to be a big boy."

"Well, I'd better go for now----just wanted to say 'hello.' I have to get back to make Brandon his lunch!"

The lady turned and walked back down the driveway.  Diane's mother wished she had asked her name, but she was already gone. Diane would probably know who she was, especially since the nice lady enjoyed Little John so much.

Diane's mother folded up the quilt, recruited Little John to help pick up his toys to place in the bag, and then went into the cottage.  She knew Diane would be returning soon, and she wanted to help her put away the grocery ties. In only a few minutes she heard Diane's car pull into the drive.

When Diane entered the back door, she said, "Mom,

did everything go OK while I was gone?" Diane started unpacking a few items that she bought at the grocery store on her way home.

"Oh, perfectly. Little John and I spent some time in the back yard on the quilt. Your nice neighbor dropped by. She said she loves watching Little John---she commented on how fast he was growing up."

"Oh, really? What was her name?"

"I'm sorry. I didn't ask her name. I figured you knew who she was. She was so nice! She commented on how fast Little John had been growing, so I thought she was surely someone you knew. And—oh—she said she had to go fix lunch for …I thought it was her husband, but she didn't really say that. She said a name----started with either a "D" or a "B" I think. Oh, I am sorry I can't remember!"

Diane didn't want to alarm her mother by telling her she didn't know whom the woman was. It seemed perfectly innocent anyway. Maybe it was the nice, elderly lady she saw three of four times since they had lived there. Out of curiosity, Diane walked to the side of the house to where the stone vase was perched on the pillar. Ahhh--she finally figured out who kept placing flowers there. Fresh–cut flowers filled the vase. It had to be that nice lady who talked to her mom!

Diane decided she'd ask around the neighborhood the first chance she got to find out the lady's name.

She wanted to write a nice 'thank-you' note. Diane asked the neighbors next door and in the next three houses down the street. The neighbors next door, the Adkins, were professional people who were on the go most of the time. They didn't have children, but there were several family members who popped in from time to time. They didn't know of any elderly woman in the neighborhood, and none of their relatives fit that description, either.

The neighbors on the other side of the Adkins were the Ritchies. They were younger and had two children still living at home.

"Yes! There is a nice, elderly neighbor in the next house over. I bet she is the one you've seen," Mrs. Ritchie said. Diane felt some relief at finally coming close to locating the mystery lady.

When Diane reached the next house, she met a very sweet little lady who only looked to weigh about 90 pounds. Diane could tell by looking that this lady was not the one she had seen several times, but she decided to ask anyway. "I'm Diane and I live in the house at the end of the street and…" Diane was interrupted in mid-sentence.

"Oh, yes! You have done a beautiful job restoring that old house. I think it looks better now than it did when it was new!" the lady exclaimed.

"Then you've been here a long time?" Diane asked.

"Oh, yes----my husband and I bought our

house when this neighborhood was brand new. He's been gone now about 23 years. I love living here, though. I don't ever want to move."

"Do you happen to know of a nice lady about your age who sometimes walks in the neighborhood?" Diane asked hoping to finally get the answer to her questions.

"No----no one left here like that. Can you tell me a little about what she looks like?" she acted genuinely interested.

"Well, every time I've seen her, she has on an apron. I think she keeps pruning shears in the front pocket. I can see the handle sticking out. She has wavy, gray hair, cut chin length, and she's about 5'4'' or so. She always wears a long skirt and sandals."

"There used to be a lady who lived in your house with her husband who fits that description, but she's been gone many, many years. It must be someone else. I'm sorry I can't help you."

Diane walked back home thinking she would ask more neighbors as time would permit. She had to get home----she had to cook dinner!

# Chapter Seven
## Thanksgiving at Home
### November 1922

The trees were turning from green to a golden color, and some were a deep-reddish orange. Some trees had already lost their leaves. Brisk winds blew leaves down the streets, accumulating in small piles near protected areas. Kids kicked the leaves tirelessly, spreading leaves every direction only to find them piled back together with one puff of the wind.

Marilyn left school early on Wednesday in order to help her mother with food preparation for Thanksgiving dinner on Thursday. All of the relatives were converging on the Davis house this year, so Marilyn and her mother were responsible for the preparation of everything. If Marilyn helped her mother from the time she arrived until the time Brandon left his office, she would be able to go to a movie with him that evening. She was so anxious to see him. Thanksgiving dinner was the perfect opportunity for Brandon to meet most of her relatives---they had already heard about him---but now they would get to meet him in person.

Marilyn and her mother worked steadily once Marilyn arrived. Between digging out the pots and pans and organizing the recipes, it gave them the perfect time to discuss Marilyn's relationship with Brandon.

"Mother, I know you and Dad want me to date several men once I complete my degree and before settling down. Oh, I dated a couple of guys in school, but most of the time I was just too busy for that. I really thought I would do that---until I met Brandon. Since being with Brandon, I don't want to be with anyone else. If I can't be with Brandon then I don't want to be with anyone. I'd rather be alone. Mom, I think there will come a day when Brandon will ask me to marry him. I want to say 'yes.' Shouldn't I say, 'yes,' Mom?"

"Of course, Marilyn," her mother said lovingly. "A woman knows when she has met the right man. She knows it in her heart. It can't be explained. Do what your heart tells you to do."

That evening, Brandon picked Marilyn up to go to the movie. They had never been to a movie together before. What was it going to be like, thought Brandon, to sit next to Marilyn but to not hold a conversation with her for the entire time? He would hold her hand and perhaps kiss her on the cheek.

"So, Marilyn, there are several movies we can see tonight, so let's choose one we both want to see." Brandon acted very serious.

In reality, there was only one movie showing. There was only one movie theater in town, so two movies were rotated daily for about two weeks until the new offerings were presented. Marilyn didn't know that.

"OK, here are the choices: *Massacre on Mustique Island*....."

"That doesn't sound too good----violent maybe," Marilyn said with a slight frown on her face.

"OK, how about *Serial Killer Strikes New York?*"

"Really, are you kidding me?" Marilyn had caught on by now.

"Then how about *"Murder in the Guest House?"*

"I was thinking about the one called *Romantic Hideaway!*

"Really? Are you kidding me?" Brandon said to mock Marilyn's earlier answer.

"Then how about *Love on a Lonely Island?"*

They went back and forth before Marilyn asked, "So what are the *real* choices?"

"OK, " Brandon whispered. "If you insist. Our choices for the 7:00 pm movie are *Peaceful Reunion* or *Peaceful Reunion."* You choose, though. It's your decision."

"Let me think---this might be a hard decision." Marilyn paused with a serious, contemplative look on her face. "I think I'd like to see *Perfect Reunion.*"

"Then it is!" Brando smiled grabbing Marilyn's hand and spinning her around in one of their famous dance moves.

When the movie ended, they talked all the way back to the Davis house. Marilyn talked about helping her mother earlier in the day but never mentioned the conversation she had with her mother concerning him.

"Are you sure you know how to make a cherry pie?" Brandon asked in a very serious tone. "And what about dressing? Are you sure you know how to cook? I don't want Thanksgiving dinner to be a flop." Brandon loved to tease.

"Well, I can't really remember how to make most of the stuff, but, *surely*, it will come out right," Marilyn commented playfully.

"There ya go, calling me *Shirley* again. You'd think the girl would learn!" Both burst out laughing. One of these days, Marilyn was not going to get suckered into that joke again. The couple sat in the living room giggling and joking until almost midnight.

"You must go to bed now. You need all of your strength to do all of that cooking tomorrow." Besides, he knew Marilyn's parents would appreciate the lack of laughter after the midnight hour. "I'll see you around 5:00. Call me if you need me to do anything to help. I'm good with salt and pepper. I can shake it with the best of 'um," Brandon said as he walked to the door. "Been practicing all my life---honing my skills."

Brandon turned around and gathered Marilyn in his arms. He held her as tightly as he could and then kissed her lips gently. His heart was beating fast, and he knew he had to turn around, or he wouldn't be able to stop. Marilyn felt the same way. Leaving each other was the hardest thing they had to do. Brandon turned to the door. Marilyn let him out then retreated to her room. Thanksgiving was going to be so much fun! There was that roller coaster feeling in her stomach again!

2

The dinner was wonderful. Marilyn and her mother prepared two turkeys, a ham, and the usual side dishes. Mashed potatoes were always a favorite dish and, of course, cornbread dressing. Fresh-cooked green beans and rice casserole were tradition. Marilyn's mom made the best homemade rolls. Since everyone had a sweet tooth at Thanksgiving, the women made one cherry pie, two pecan pies, and two pumpkin pies. Fresh whipped cream was cooled in the refrigerator and was the perfect topping for the pies. The fruit salad that they prepared for dinner was eaten as dessert by those who put a dollop of whipped cream on top.

After dinner, the children went to the bedroom to play games while the adults retreated to the living room for after-dinner drinks and conversation.

Everyone really enjoyed meeting Brandon. He was as charming and as funny as he had always been. The Davises were quite proud of this young man who was with their daughter. Aunt Linda was beaming.

And, of course, Brandon came out with one of his jokes:

*"A man was pulled over by the police at 2:00 a.m. for weaving down the road. The police officer asked the man, "What are you doing at 2:00 in the morning driving this way---you are intoxicated!"*

*"W-w-well, officer, I'm g-g-going to a l-l-lecture" the man said slurring his words.*

*"Really? You are going to a lecture at 2:00 in the morning? What kind of lecture is it?"*

*"Oh, it's a l-l-l-lecture about the h-h-h-hazards of drinkin' and drivin' and staying out late--'n even s-s-smoking----and not takin' care of your b-b-body."*

*"Really! And who is giving this lecture at 2:00 in the morning?" the officer asked.*

*"Th-th-th-that would be m-m-my wife!" the man slurred.*

Brandon was already a hit with the family and laughter rang out with that one!

Marilyn and Brandon had three more days before she had to return to school. They made the most of every day. Of course, dancing would take up their Saturday night. There wasn't a contest this weekend, but they would have just as much fun.

"Brandon?" Marilyn asked. "There are only 18 days until I'm back. Then I'll be home for almost one month. I hope you don't get tired of me!"

"Well, that *is* a little bit much. Maybe we can call up ol' Mark to see if he'll take you out and give me a break!" Brandon said jokingly. Brandon remembered that Mark was the young attorney that Marilyn had met at her father's law office. He also remembered that she accepted a date with Mark and their picture appeared in the local newspaper. Brandon could joke about it now because there was *no way* he would ever allow Marilyn to be with anyone else---not now---not ever.

"Oh, certainly," Marilyn was going to go right along with him. "We made a nice couple, don't you think? And I think it was a particularly good picture of us together in the paper, too. Don't y think?" Brandon made a face at that comment.

"We're going to be so busy in December that you won't have one minute to be with anyone else. As many surprises as we have in our lives,

I'm sure there will be one in December, too," Brandon said.

Marilyn thought the surprise could just be about anything, but she secretively hoped Brandon would start a conversation with her about someday getting married. She certainly didn't expect a proposal or a ring, but she thought they might at least discuss the topic.

Marilyn felt several good things happened this Thanksgiving besides the fact that she got to be with Brandon. She proved to him that she was able to cook and bake—a very good thing to know. And, most of her relatives had the opportunity to meet Brandon for the first time. It was a successful day. Sunday night would be her last night at home, and then she would have to drive back. The thought of it gave Marilyn a sinking feeling.

4

"Marilyn," her mother said as she cleaned up the dishes after lunch the next day. "Your father and I must go to Frisco tomorrow. Your Aunt Gena isn't doing well, and your father and I want to try to help her if we possibly can. We will need to drive there in the morning, but we won't be able to get back until the following day. I'm so sorry that we're taking this precious time away from you, but we had no warning. I know you'll understand. There's plenty of food left over from our Thanksgiving dinner and much more in the freezer if you get tired of turkey. You should have Brandon over while we're gone."

"What's wrong with Aunt Gena?"

"She had a pretty bad fall, and she's now in the hospital. We need to go check on her and then find a rehabilitation center where she can recover. I know her doctor will have some advice and a recommendation, but we need to see for ourselves. I'm afraid she's at the age where we need to find a nursing care facility for her."

"I understand. Oh, don't worry about me one bit. I'll be fine, and I do have quite a bit of work to do to get ready for my final exams in December. Plus, I really want to spend as much time with Brandon as I can while I'm here."

As her mother scurried around getting things ready for the trip the next morning, Marilyn placed a phone call to Brandon at his office.

"Remington office," the secretary said cheerfully as she answered the phone.

"Hi, Sandy, this is Marilyn Davis. Is Brandon there? May I speak to him?"

"Oh, hi Marilyn. He is with a client right at the moment, but I'll tell him you called as soon as he gets free."

"Thanks. I really appreciate it." Marilyn was disappointed that she couldn't speak to Brandon, but she knew he would call back as soon as he got a chance.

In less than thirty minutes, the phone rang at the Davis house. Marilyn answered immediately. "Hello?"

Brandon was on the other end of the line. "Marilyn? Is that you? Is that really you? Calling for me?"

"Yes, and I have called you before so why the big surprise?"

"Well----because rumor has it that you had lunch with Mark, and then you went shopping with him, and then y'all went to a movie and then…."

"Yeah, sure Mr. Remington. That really happened. In fact, why am I calling you now? Since I forgot, I'll just hang up right now!"

"Wait! Wait! Waaaaaiiitt! Don't hang up. I'm sure you'll be able to think of the reason you called. *Please*." Brandon knew they were just playing a little game.

"Well, what would you say if I told you my parents were going out of town tomorrow night, and I wanted to have dinner with you at my house? There is plenty of food as you well know! It will just be the two of us!"

"Oh! That would be great! I know that's the last night we'll have together until the Christmas break, so that would be very special. I'll be there."

Brandon hung up the phone and smiled. He had planned on being with Marilyn that evening, but it was going to involve dining out and perhaps going for a walk. Now, they would be alone together, and it would be special. But---he didn't know exactly how special it was going to be. Neither did she.

5

Marilyn's parents packed the car to head out early the next morning. After kisses all around, they waved goodbye and backed the car out of the driveway. Marilyn told them to be careful and then turned to go back into the house. She had some errands to run but would be home early in order to pull together a fabulous dinner for Brandon. She wouldn't really have to do much cooking since there were so many leftovers in the refrigerator. She really only had to warm up the food. She set the table and placed a special bowl of flowers in the center. She wanted everything to look perfect for Brandon. After all, that was going to be the last night they would see each other for a while. She would have to leave the next day for the university.

Brandon arrived early---he just couldn't wait any longer to see her. Figuring that to be the case, Marilyn had everything ready to go when he arrived.

"Wow, what a feast!" he exclaimed looking over the dishes on the table. He loved turkey and dressing, especially when Marilyn had prepared it. But she had all of the side dishes to go along with it! Mashed-potatoes and gravy? *Now that is a man's meal!* he thought.

After a wonderful meal with plenty of stories, jokes and laughter, the conversation turned very serious.

"Marilyn, you make me the happiest man in the world. I love every minute that I get to spend with you. When I'm with you, I'm a very happy person. When I'm not with you, I'm either thinking about you, or I'm sad because I can't be with you."

"I feel the same way, Brandon. I really do. But I don't want to be sad tonight. We have this time together, and I want it to be happy."

"I do, too. Here, let's pick up these dishes and get this place cleaned up." He stood up and started gathering all of the dishes and leftover food. As Marilyn put away the food, he started washing the dishes. She picked up the dishtowel and started drying.

"We do make a pretty good team, don't you think?" Brandon said as he handed her a dripping platter.

"Couldn't be better!" A large smile came to her face, and she leaned a little closer to Brandon. Just being a little closer brought the warmest feeling to Brandon. He detected a slight increase in his heartbeat and a burning desire to throw his arms around her---wet hands or not.

Marilyn felt the same way. She couldn't believe

this handsome man was standing so close to her, and he was washing dishes!  She loved him so much.

After the dishes were put away, Brandon held her hand to walk her to the living room.  Sitting down on the sofa, Brandon thanked her for such a lovely meal and then moved a little closer to her.  He couldn't resist.  He enveloped her in his arms and kissed her lips ever so softly.  It was a long kiss---a meaningful kiss----a kiss that told her how he wanted her.  She melted into the kiss.  She loved his arms holding her and caressing her.  Her head leaned into his neck and she kissed him tenderly.  No words were said.  No words needed to be said.

More than anything, Brandon wanted to be with her for the rest of his life.  He made up his mind at that instant.  "Marilyn…..Marilyn……Marilyn…….I love you so very much."  Then they both fell asleep in each other's arms.  Marilyn felt that she was in heaven.  Brandon did, too.  This was a wonderful, wonderful world.

Chapter Eight
Getting Serious
December 1932


Brandon made a decision over the Thanksgiving holiday. He already knew he wanted to marry Marilyn but felt there was no real reason to wait any longer than necessary. He will find just the right ring, will ask Mr. Davis for Marilyn's hand, and then he will ask Marilyn to marry him. If she agrees, they will be engaged during her second semester at school and then, after graduation, they will get married. He will talk to Mr. and Mrs. Davis in December, right before Marilyn gets home. Originally, he was going to wait to propose until after she graduated but then their engagement would be short, or at least if Brandon had any say in the matter. Proposing in December will be a complete surprise to Marilyn, but it will also give her five months to work on the wedding, if a date in June is chosen.

Brandon thought about the idea of marrying Marilyn over and over. He wanted everything to be perfect. He wanted to ask her parents for her hand in just the right way, and he wanted to propose to her in just the right way. Then Brandon wanted to have just the right house for them to move into.

The only thing Brandon worried about was Marilyn's career. She had always wanted to belong to a dance troupe and perform around the world---or so he thought. There would be no way for Brandon to leave his career. Once Marilyn mentioned that she could teach dance, perhaps own her own dance studio, and still participate in performances in a very limited basis. She could also teach voice lessons. Her career goals seemed to change once she met Brandon. He decided he would write her, asking clarification about her career dreams.

*Dear Marilyn,*

*Thanksgiving was excellent in every way. The dinner was delicious. Now, I know you can cook! Your mother is a wonderful cook, so I know you have a good teacher. I'm pretty talented with boiling water, so I can teach you that anytime you are ready. Not to mention the salt and pepper thing.*

*Our dinner together at your house was truly unbelievable. I can't describe the evening. There are no words that even come close to explaining how I felt holding you in my arms. I want us to spend the rest of our lives together.*

*You once mentioned that you wanted to join a dance troupe and tour the world. Is that still a career goal? I'm trying to prepare myself for after your graduation. If that is still your ambition, does that mean I'll see you less than I do now? Do I need to start drinking heavily, so I can deal with this? If this is no longer your plan, then what would you like to do? I love you so much.*

*Love,*
*Brandon*

Marilyn's response came fairly quickly.

*Dear Brandon,*

*I have been terribly busy this week. After classes each day, I head for the arts building to rehearse. There is so much singing and dancing---none as much fun as what we do together, but I enjoy it. Rehearsals sometimes last until 10:00 pm. This schedule is really tiring! It makes the days go by quickly, but that is a good thing.*

*Brandon, I decided some time ago that I would not be traveling with a dance troupe or singing in performances across the country after I graduate. As long as we are together, I'm going to be near you. I can always teach voice and dance and be perfectly happy. When I graduate, I'll be in Slaton on a permanent basis, that is, if you let me be a part of your life. If not, I'll see what Mark is interested in doing. HA HA.*

*Love,*
*Marilyn*

2

When Brandon received Marilyn's reply, he didn't need anything else to move forward with his plans. He was so anxious to see her for Christmas break, but now he had a lot of work to do. Being organized, Brandon made out a 'to-do' list to follow:

Tell parents about plan of action.
Tell Bonnie about plan of action.
Ask Bonnie to help with the ring and proposal.
Decide on proposal.
Talk to Marilyn's parents before she arrives.
The Perfect Proposal.

Brandon had only 18 days to get everything done. He decided he would recruit Bonnie to help as soon as he discussed his plans with his parents. One day after dinner, Brandon told them he had something very important to discuss.

"You know, Marilyn and I've been dating since May. You also know that I'm totally in love with her. I promised her parents that I wouldn't interfere with her finishing her degree. I'll keep that promise. What would you think if I propose to Marilyn when she's here for Christmas? It would be with the understanding that the wedding wouldn't take place until after she graduates," Brandon said.

"That sounds like a wonderful plan, son," his father said. "We think the world of Marilyn," His father continued. "I think the two of you are perfect for each other."

"I can't think of a lovelier or sweeter girl to have as a daughter-in-law!" Brandon's mother chimed in. She was overwhelmed with happiness for her son.

"I'm going to get Bonnie to help me with this. She'll be great," Brandon said. He knew he only had to get through the proposal. Then Marilyn would take over and do the rest of the planning. Not once did Brandon think she wouldn't accept his proposal.

When Bonnie got in from her meeting, Brandon cornered her in the kitchen. "You always wanted a sister, didn't ya?" Brandon said coyly.

It took a second or two for Bonnie to figure out what he was talking about. Then she screamed and did a little dance in the room.

"Are you kidding? Really, are you kidding? Are you giving up your title of Most Eligible Bachelor? I can't believe it! I'll alert the media!"

Then Bonnie asked questions so quickly Brandon couldn't get a word in to interrupt. "Have you proposed yet? What did she say? What did Mom and Dad say? Do you have a ring yet?"

"No, I haven't proposed, yet. We haven't even talked about getting married, yet. You don't get anything for free in this world so in order for you to get a sister-in-law, you have to pay the price," Brandon said making a deal.

"You want ME to propose to her?" Bonnie said jokingly.

"Oh, sure. That would work well, don't ya think?" Brandon said sarcastically. "Dearest

Marilyn, my brother loves you more than anything in the whole world. Will you marry him?" Brandon said as if Bonnie were saying it. They both laughed hysterically.

"OK, smartie pie----what do I have to do?" she asked.

"I need you to do two things. <u>First</u>, I need you to help me find the right ring and <u>second</u>, I need you to help me decide how to propose. You always have good ideas," Brandon said. "But, it is very, very important that you keep this secret."

"I have some questions," Bonnie said mimicking Brandon. "<u>First</u>, are you going to buy the ring before you discuss marriage with Marilyn? And, <u>second</u>, what if she says, 'No'?"

"<u>First</u> of all----I know her and <u>second</u> of all--I know her," Brandon answered with confidence.

3

Bonnie was thrilled and was so excited to be such an important player in the surprise. She also thought Marilyn was perfect for Brandon. They decided that Bonnie would look for the ring. Since everyone knew Brandon, it would cause quite a stir and considerable gossip if he went looking for an engagement ring.

Bonnie was also given the assignment of thinking up creative ways for Brandon to propose to

Marilyn. He waited to hear what ideas she had. She had several great, creative ideas.

"OK, you could have another private dinner at the same restaurant that Aunt Linda had arranged for y'all. You could hide the ring in a flower and when Marilyn discovers it, you could get down on one knee and propose. It would be very romantic and totally private."

Brandon decided against that idea saying that they had been there before. He thought it was beautiful and romantic, but he wanted something totally different.

Bonnie had another idea. "OK, what if you propose to Marilyn on stage at the Slaton Christmas Pageant? Marilyn has a singing part in the production. It could be arranged that Marilyn would get a door prize at the end of the event. When she comes back on stage to receive the prize, she would be presented with a rather large box. Inside that box would be another box and then another until it finally got down to one small jewelry box----the box that houses the engagement ring. When Marilyn sees the ring, she'll be so surprised. Then the presenter will ask her to turn around. You could hide in one of the large cubes that is made up to look like a giant Christmas present. Marilyn could be positioned with her back to the cube. At that instant, you will appear from inside the giant present and will get down on one knee. Marilyn will realize what is happening and will be overwhelmed with joy. Everyone will cheer!"

Bonnie thought it was a grand idea. Brandon didn't. He didn't want the proposal to be so public. "Can't you think of something a little more private?" Brandon pleaded.

"OK," Bonnie said calmly. "I know just the perfect plan. Tell Marilyn you want to take her on a horse and carriage ride. You know how we have those special carriage rides at Christmas? I love the black carriage that is drawn by the solid white horse. How beautiful he is! The two of you can bundle up with mom's, cuddly winter throw as the carriage takes you to see the Christmas lights around town. You know it goes down by the creek and park, too. Then, we can arrange for your driver to take you to the fountain down on the town square. It is so beautifully lit that time of year. You two could get out to throw coins in the fountain and then you can propose to her right there. If she says 'Yes" you can tell her your wish came true. If she says 'No', well it's back to the drawing board for you ol' man---or you can throw her into the fountain." Bonnie laughed.

Ignoring the last statement, "That's a plan!" Brandon said. "I think that is perfect. Then I can have the driver take us to her parent's home to show them her ring. They'll already know about the proposal because I'll tell them earlier on Friday.

"Great!" Bonnie said enthusiastically. "I'll start working on it right away!"

"Just one more thing," Brandon added. "Don't tell a soul. I don't want anyone to know anything about this. I'll ask Marilyn's father for her hand right before she gets home. I want everything to be perfect."

Marilyn jotted down a few notes on a small, yellow piece of paper. It was a cheat sheet for Brandon to use. "Here," Bonnie said. "This is for good luck." It said:

Pick up ring.
Put ring in pocket.
Get down on one knee.
Ask Marilyn to marry you.
Kiss her.

4

Bonnie went to the two jewelry stores in a larger, neighboring town, looking at all of the rings. She had to be the scout. Since Brandon was so well known around nearby Slaton and had been considered the most eligible bachelor, word would travel fast, and there would be a chance that Marilyn could hear about it. Bonnie visited several jewelry stores including those in Clarkstown before finding the perfect ring. It was a beautiful princess cut diamond in a platinum gold band. It was exquisite! If Brandon liked it, all it needed was proper sizing and it would be ready. Bonnie thought it was the most beautiful ring she'd ever seen.

When Brandon saw the ring, he instantly liked it.

He liked the way it sparkled. He didn't know Marilyn's exact ring size but figured her mother could help with that. Then, Bonnie pointed out, how could they get the ring size from Mrs. Davis without letting out the secret. Even if they didn't say it was for an engagement ring, or if they said it was for a 'ring' the Davises would be very suspicious. Brandon and Bonnie decided to get the size as close as possible and have it sized after the proposal if needed. OK—that is the safest thing, they decided.

Brandon planned the days carefully so that everything would fall into place smoothly.

"Bonnie, I'll be taking Mom and Dad to visit Aunt Joyce and Uncle Clarence for a few days before Marilyn comes in. Will you make sure you pick up the ring sometime before Friday? Maybe you should pick it up either Wednesday or Thursday, just to make sure the correct dates are engraved in the ring. The first date, is the date we first met, May 27, 1932. The second date is the date we are getting engaged, December 13, 1932. If you pick the ring up early, there's still time to correct the dates if they're incorrect," Brandon carefully explained. "We'll return on Thursday evening late. I'll meet with the Davises on Friday afternoon---hopefully---to ask their daughter's hand in marriage."

"And if they say 'no?' Bonnie teased. Brandon just glared at her. "I'm just saying....it's possible....anything's possible...."

Chapter Nine
Days Before the Proposal
December 1932

Brandon's plan was to just drop by the Davis house before Marilyn was to arrive. He knew they would both be home. They wouldn't think anything of him dropping by since he usually did that when Marilyn was coming in from college. Everything was going to go smoothly, he was convinced.

Brandon drove his parents to visit his aunt and uncle who lived in Abernathy, a small town approximately three hours from Slaton. They had a wonderful time on their visit.

"Brandon, I hear that you have found quite a lovely young lady who you are very interested in," Aunt Joyce said.

"Yes, Aunt Joyce. I think Marilyn is the perfect person for me. I've dated many girls over the last few years, and none of them can compare to Marilyn. If the proposal works like I hope it will, I'll be engaged by Friday evening," Brandon responded proudly.

"This is so exciting, Brandon," Aunt Joyce said cheerfully. "I can't wait to hear how everything goes Friday night!"

"We can't get married until after Marilyn finishes the second semester, but she'll probably want a summer wedding anyway," Brandon commented with a smile on his face. "I promised her parents she *would* finish her degree." Brandon was determined that nothing would get in the way of doing just that.

Brandon and his parents had a wonderful time visiting his aunt and uncle. They even planned what all they would do when all the relatives come in for the wedding. They made a mental list of the relatives they needed to invite.

"We mustn't forget to ask cousin John," Aunt Joyce said seriously. "Remember? Albert forgot to send him an invitation to his wedding and it caused a rift in the family!"

"Oh! I remember that!" Brandon's mother exclaimed. "Maybe we should start writing a list while we are all together. I'd hate to do this on my own!"

So, the wedding planning began----at least the invitation list. Brandon got a kick out of listening to his mother, father, aunt, and uncle discussing which family members should be invited and which shouldn't. Even his father threw in an opinion or two.

"Let's be sure to invite all the people who were good to Brandon when he was just starting his business."

Then Brandon's mother and aunt started whispering so that the men couldn't hear.

"Oh, come on ladies----let us in on what you're saying!"

"Well, we were just discussing what is going to happen when we invite Robert Barnett and his three wives show up! We have to invite them, because they would be totally hurt and embarrassed if we don't!"

"Then I think I'll just sit back and watch this happen." Brandon's father said crossing his hands across his chest and leaning back slightly in his chair.

"Oohh...I can see that this can get a little sticky," Brandon added. "Making this list is going to be a little more difficult than I thought."

Brandon was thankful that he took the time from work to go on this short trip with his parents. He had been so busy over the last few years that he didn't make that much time for them. Since he still lived at home, he saw them almost every day, but it was usually on his way in or out of the house. Spending some quality time with them was a good thing, he thought. He had not seen his aunt and uncle either, for quite some time. As Brandon grew older, and especially since he was going to get married and start a family of his own, he valued family more and more.

Everyone had such a wonderful time that the

evening slipped up on them. They wanted to get an earlier start home. As it turns out, those precious extra minutes would be treasured by Aunt Joyce and Uncle Clarence for the rest of their lives.

2

It was a crystal-clear night. The earlier threat of thunderstorms had disappeared and the sky was calm. Brandon and his parents joked and laughed on their way home. Additional plans were made for the rehearsal dinner as Brandon got more and more excited. After all, tomorrow was going to be one of the most exciting and one of the most important days of his life. He couldn't wait to see Marilyn. Their lives together had been one surprise after the other but proposing marriage to her Friday was going to be the grandfather of all surprises! How exciting!

"Brandon, have you decided how you are going to propose to Marilyn?" his mother asked.

"Oh, certainly! Bonnie worked it all out for me. She found a fantastic ring and had it engraved. I'm going to take Marilyn on a carriage ride to see the lights and the fountain on the square. When we stop at the fountain, I'm going to propose to her there. If she says 'yes' we'll go over to her parents' home to tell them. Of course, I'm going to ask them ahead of time. I hope to talk to them before Marilyn gets home tomorrow."

"I'm happy for you, hon," his mother said. "I think Marilyn is a wonderful young woman.

Your dad and I both believe that. And, it's obvious how much she loves you. When she's with you, her eyes sparkle!"

"Tomorrow is going to be a very significant day for me! Brandon said grinning from ear to ear.

"Brandon," his father said, "I guess the wedding will be sometime next summer?"

As Brandon nodded, his mother said, "You don't know that----Marilyn will pick the right date with your help I'm sure. She has to get out of school first and then there's a lot of planning to do, so I'm not sure when she'll be ready."

"The reason I'm asking about that is I've heard that the Adkins family is moving to Colorado after school is out. Their house will be up for sale soon, and that house is beautiful. I've seen it myself. Brandon---should we look into that pretty soon?"

"Sounds good to me, Dad." Brandon said, "Maybe I can show the house to Marilyn while she's here for the holidays." Things were really beginning to fall into place.

3

*Lives have a way of changing in a split second.* Just as their car came over a small incline in the road, a large truck crossed the middle stripe of the road, crashing headfirst into the Remington's car. It happened in a split second. There was no way to avoid the accident. In fact, it is quite possible that they never even knew what hit them. Brandon's father was driving and his mother was in the front passenger seat. Brandon was in the backseat, a fact that probably saved him from instant death.

People coming upon the terrible wreck immediately sent for an ambulance. They feared the very worst. They couldn't see how any of the occupants in the car or truck could be alive. The car was crushed by the impact. By the time the ambulance arrived, there were two local police cars and several bystanders who had come upon the scene.

"Oh! Pray to God for those poor souls," one bystander said to another. "What a tragedy right here before Christmas."

"Do you know how many people were in the car?" one man asked.

"No, the car is so mangled. They are still trying to get to the people."

The sky was pitch black. Flashing, red lights alerted oncoming drivers that a terrible accident had occurred. Others had flashlights that were aimed at the scene. Sadness filled the air. The night was somber. Strangers could be heard sniffling, as they were overcome by the emotion of tragedy and what they were witness to. People whispered, as to not disturb the emergency workers who were yelling orders out to each other. They had to pry the doors off the car in order to get inside. By the look of the car and truck, no one could possibly be alive. But everyone had to be sure. They were doing everything possible to get to the injured as soon as possible.

The police in Slaton were notified as soon as identification was made of the accident victims.

"Officer Johnson?" the policeman on the other end of the phone asked.

"Yes, this is Johnson," he answered.

"There's been a terrible accident here in Grayson County off farm road 4133 and three of your townsfolk were….were…. injured pretty badly. They were in a terrible crash---- a terrible crash."

"Oh! No! Who do you have?" Officer Johnson questioned downheartedly.

"Well, do you know the Remington family?" he asked.

"Yes---they are outstanding community members. I know the whole family. Please tell me it's not as bad as you sound."

"I'm sorry. It was quite a tragic accident. Mr. and Mrs. Remington probably died instantly. Their son, Brandon, was riding in the back seat. He's in critical condition and is not expected to live through the night. He sustained a very serious head injury."

"Oh, no!  How did it happen?"

"As far as we can tell, a large truck crossed the center stripe and crashed head-on into their car just as they came over a slight incline.  They probably didn't even see it coming.  Hope not.  We don't know if the trucker fell asleep or had a heart attack or what.  Terrible thing---just terrible.  He died, too."

"That young man clinging to his life is one of our community's shining stars---can't do enough to help everyone.  He's young, too----mid 20's I think.  He has a sister---still lives at home---she's maybe two or three years younger.  I'll need to get to her immediately.  Oh, God.  Help us."

4

Officer Johnson drove to the Remington home.  By now it was close to 10:00 pm.  He rang the doorbell and waited.  Bonnie was still up reading; she peered out the window of her bedroom.  When she saw the police car, she wondered why the officer was dropping by the Remington house so late.  Was something going on in the neighborhood she wondered?

Officer Johnson brought along the minister of the church where the Remingtons attended services.  The minister's wife also came along to stay with Bonnie until other relatives could be notified.

When Bonnie opened the front door and saw the

three of them standing there, she knew something terrible had happened. It was only then that she wondered about her parents and their drive home that evening. Bonnie just stared at the trio and said, "What? What has happened? Please don't tell me…" her voice faded off.

"Bonnie, there's been a terrible accident. Your parents were in a terrible wreck. Honey, your parents didn't make it. They lost their lives in that wreck."

Bonnie screamed and fell to the floor. She felt herself go completely numb. It was like it was a dream----*Did she hear that right? They died? It can't be. It can't be. They were supposed to come home tonight.* "And Brandon?" Bonnie cried hysterically. The minister's wife held Bonnie in her arms the entire time.

"Bonnie?" Officer Johnson said softly. "Your brother is in the hospital. He's been hurt pretty badly but he's alive….now…..but…." Bonnie couldn't comprehend what was being told to her. She couldn't think. She had to get to the hospital as soon as possible. Then she remembered Marilyn.

"Oh my gosh!" Bonnie cried out. "You have to tell the Davises. You have to tell them! Their daughter is coming in tomorrow afternoon to be with my brother. She can't hear this from anyone else while she's at school."

The officer got the address from Bonnie and left to talk to Mr. and Mrs. Davis. The minister and his wife stayed with Bonnie as she grabbed a few items to take with her to the hospital. They drove her the 90 or so minutes to the hospital where Brandon was. They knew Brandon's chances of survival were slim, but they had seen miracles before. They didn't tell Bonnie. On the way, Bonnie explained how Brandon and Marilyn loved each other, but she never mentioned the proposal plans she and Brandon had made together. She never mentioned the ring or the carriage ride or the proposal. Just yesterday, Bonnie had picked up the ring. It was absolutely beautiful and dates were accurate: May 28, 1932 and December 13, 1932.

The ring sat in a box in Bonnie's dresser drawer. Bonnie would show it to Brandon later, she thought, once he recovered and got out of the hospital.

5

When Officer Johnson knocked on the Davis's front door, it was close to 11:45 pm. When Mr. Davis answered the door and saw Officer Johnson, he absolutely thought the worst---he thought something had happened to Marilyn.

"Mr. Davis, I was told to come here by Bonnie Remington. There has been a terrible accident and her parents have been killed." The Davises gasped and held on to each other. "Their son, Brandon, was also in the car but he is in the hospital."

"Oh no! Is he all right? Is he all right?" Mrs. Davis screamed. "Please tell me he is all right!"

"He's being cared for by the best doctors around. The minister and his wife are taking his sister Bonnie to the hospital right now. She asked that we tell you. Brandon's in pretty bad shape. He might not make it."

"No---no! Our daughter is in love with Brandon and he is her entire life. Please, God, please take care of Brandon," Mrs. Davis cried out with tears streaming down her face. "Marilyn is supposed to drive in tomorrow after her last final exam, but we must get to her tonight. She'll want to go to the hospital immediately."

Trying to figure out the quickest way to get Marilyn to the hospital, Mr. Davis said, "If we drive down to get her, it will take 4 hours and then another 5 1/2 to get back home and then to the hospital. That might be too late. Why don't we ask her friend, Carrie, to drive her. I certainly don't want her driving herself in such an emotional state. In fact, we mustn't tell her about anything until we are with her. I'll call Carrie right now."

Mr. Davis didn't really want Carrie to drive either, but it was a desperate situation.

Mr. Davis called the campus security department and explained the emergency. They contacted the dorm mother, Miss Rita, who called Mr. Davis for the information. She got Carrie on the phone for the call from Mr. Davis.

"Carrie?" Mr. Davis said apologetically. "This is Marilyn's father. I'm very sorry to be calling you at this hour, but I desperately need your help. Marilyn's boyfriend Brandon…" Mr. Davis paused to catch his breath. "Brandon has been in a terrible car wreck, and he is in the hospital in Brownwood, about an hour and a half from here. I know Marilyn will want to go to the hospital as soon as possible. If we drive to get her, it'll take another four hours. If you drive her, perhaps you could start right away. I can't allow Marilyn to drive by herself."

Carrie could feel the urgency in Mr. Davis's voice. It scared her. "Of course, we will leave immediately. Are you going to talk to Marilyn now?"

"Yes, if you'll just tell her she has a call, I'll stay on the line."

Carrie went up to Marilyn's room and tapped on the door. "Marilyn, you have a call," Carrie said then followed Marilyn down the hall.

"Why are you telling me? Did Miss Bryan send you after me? Who's calling?" Marilyn thought it was so strange to get a call that late at night and why was Carrie involved?

"Hello?" Marilyn answered.

"Marilyn," her father said. "I just talked to

Carrie. She is going to drive you home right now. Brandon has been in a car wreck, and he is in a hospital about an hour and a half from here. When you get here, we'll all go together. I just didn't want you to drive yourself. You wouldn't be able to keep your mind on the road."

"Daddy! Daddy! Is Brandon going to be OK? What happened? Is he going to be OK? I need to know. I really need to know," Marilyn asked so quickly that all the questions rolled together.

"I'm sure he's going to be fine," he said trying to speak in a calm voice. "I just knew you would want to see him tonight if possible."

Marilyn could put two and two together. If Brandon was hurt, but it wasn't too bad, her father would have probably waited to tell her in the morning or even after she arrived home, having completed her last final. He would have told her that Brandon had been in a car wreck, but he is fine. He would have said that Brandon got a little banged up, but that the doctors were taking good care of him, and that she should go ahead and finish her exams, so that she wouldn't leave anything incomplete. Marilyn analyzed the situation carefully. The fact that her parents wanted her home immediately was alarming to her.

Carrie didn't know anything more than what Mr. Davis had said so she couldn't offer Marilyn any information. Carrie didn't know and Marilyn didn't know that Brandon's parents had been killed. They would get that news once Marilyn reached home.

Carrie and Marilyn threw their bags in the car and headed for Slaton. They were basically packed already since both planned to leave for their respective homes the next day. A million things swirled through Marilyn's mind. *Brandon would be all right. He would absolutely be all right. He had to be,* she thought. She loved him more than anything in the world.

Four hours later when Marilyn and Carrie arrived at the Davis home, Mr. and Mrs. Davis met them at the door, ready to go. Marilyn could see the anxiety in their eyes.

"Marilyn, one of the reasons we wanted you to come right away is that we didn't want you to hear about the accident from someone else. Brandon's parents died in the wreck," her father said.

"No---no---no!" Marilyn screamed. "Oh no!" is all she could say. "Tell me. How badly did Brandon get hurt? Please tell me!" Now Marilyn was crying and pacing back and forth in the room.

"Brandon was hurt, but he's in the hospital and they're taking good care of him," Mr. Davis added.

"Let's go right now! Marilyn said hurriedly. "I need to be with Brandon."

The four of them rushed out of the door. The drive

seemed like an eternity, especially for Marilyn. All she could think about was how devastated Brandon would be over his parent's death. She would help him through his sorrow and would be there for Bonnie also. What Marilyn didn't know was how injured Brandon was. It never entered her mind that he might not make it.

6

When the Davises arrived at the hospital, Bonnie had already been there for several hours. Bonnie wouldn't leave her brother's side. Brandon was in a coma; he was connected to all kinds of tubes and electronic monitors. A doctor gave Bonnie a light sedative to help her with her trauma. Nothing really helped. Now her focus was on her brother and helping him survive. She worried about Marilyn and replayed in her mind all the events that were supposed to take place Friday evening. No one else knew that Brandon was going to propose to Marilyn during a horse-drawn carriage ride. No one else knew about the ring that Bonnie had in her dresser drawer. The first date engraved on the inside was the date Brandon and Marilyn first met. The second date, 12-13-1932 was supposed to be the date of the proposal. It would be forever wrong. Now, instead of the horse-drawn carriage ride to the fountain, Brandon was fighting for his life in the intensive care unit of Mercy General Hospital. Everything was a blur for Bonnie. She cried gently but continuously for hours until she could cry no more.

When the Davises arrived at the hospital, Marilyn and Carrie ran to the intensive care area. Upon entering the section where Brandon was lying, Marilyn gasped in horror. Overcome with grief, Marilyn lay across Brandon's legs crying. Seeing him hooked up to several monitors, she realized the extreme seriousness of his injury. Bonnie reached over to hug Marilyn and they cried together.

It was at that point that the doctor walked in. The room fell completely silent. Every eye was on Dr. Stratman. He looked very somber. That frightened Marilyn even more.

"Please, doctor," Marilyn begged. "Is Brandon going to be OK? He just has to be." She covered her face with her hands and sobbed uncontrollably.

After a long pause, and after Marilyn caught her breath, the doctor said, "Brandon sustained a very serious head and neck injury. His spinal column has been traumatized, and it may have sustained some permanent damage. We won't know for sure until we're able to do more tests. Right now, we're trying to keep him stabilized. It's really an hour to hour situation at this point."

Marilyn couldn't take her eyes off Brandon. She thought to herself, *My poor baby, I'm so sorry about your mother and father. You don't even know about that yet. I'll never leave your side. No matter what, I'll never leave your side.* Marilyn closed her eyes and prayed. Everyone prayed for Brandon and prayed for God to help Bonnie through the loss of her parents. In just a matter of an hour or so, an extensive prayer chain had formed in Slaton as the community members heard of the accident. They prayed for God to let Brandon live and prayed for the souls of his parents.

The Davises made arrangements for Bonnie and Marilyn to stay in a local boarding house while Brandon remained in the hospital there. Once he could be moved, he would be transported back to the hospital in Slaton. Mr. Davis took Carrie to the train station and bought her ticket to return to their home where her car was parked. He couldn't thank Carrie enough for driving Marilyn home that tragic night.

"I want to thank you for being there for Marilyn. Her mother and I wouldn't know what we would have done if you hadn't been there to drive Marilyn home."

It was up to Bonnie and her Aunt Joyce to make funeral arrangements for her parents. What a horrible irony, she thought. She was making wedding arrangements one day and funeral arrangements almost the next. She let Aunt Joyce make most of the arrangements since Bonnie was so tied to Brandon's bedside. Then she realized that her parents didn't know about the proposal either. Although Brandon told them he was going to ask Marilyn to marry him, they didn't know when or where it was going to happen. Brandon planned on telling them after he met with Marilyn's parents. Now, they would never know.

Many times during their stay in the hospital, Bonnie thought about telling Marilyn about the proposal plans, but she couldn't. Bonnie thought it would just be too painful. Besides, when Brandon got out of the hospital, he would want to surprise Marilyn in the same way. Bonnie didn't want to spoil that for him.

The doctors feared that Brandon wouldn't make it through the first night--- but he did. He was still in a coma when his parents' funeral took place. Bonnie attended the funeral, but Marilyn would not leave Brandon's side.

"Miss Davis," the doctor said as he entered the room. "Brandon appears to be stable, but there has been no response to some of the tests we've done. Now that he can be transported, we need to get him to the medical center in Dallas. They have the equipment and instruments that we don't have here."

Marilyn rode with Brandon in the ambulance as he was transported to the Dallas Medical Center. Marilyn spoke to Brandon every step of the way, explaining to him what was going on. She didn't know if he could hear her or if he understood her, but she knew if he could, he would appreciate it.

One evening, Marilyn whispered gently in Brandon's ear, "Darling, you've been in an accident and you are still in the hospital. If you can hear me, please move your hand. I'm holding your hand, so I can feel it if you move it." Marilyn repeated her request. There was no response. Marilyn continued talking to Brandon every day. She knew in her heart that he would wake up someday, and they could continue with their lives. She prayed more than she had ever prayed before.

When Marilyn's professors heard of the accident, they made arrangements for Marilyn to finish her course requirements. She only needed to complete two final exams, and she would be finished. The exams were mailed to Marilyn, and she was able to take them while sitting next to Brandon's bedside. She had made a promise to her parents and also to Brandon that she'd complete her degree. Now, that was behind her.

The best specialists in the world analyzed Brandon's condition. The lead doctor met with Bonnie and Marilyn one morning to discuss the prognosis. "We've done everything we can do for Brandon. He's had the best care and the best medicine that science can provide. There's nothing else for us to do---it's between God and Brandon now. He needs to be moved out of the hospital and into a nursing care center. He could be moved home, but he'll need some extensive care. There's a feeding tube that takes care and then his daily hygiene. It's just too difficult for family members to do.

## Chapter Ten
## Brandon's Slow Return

The Davises helped Marilyn and Bonnie search for the right place for Brandon. They moved him to Slaton, so that everyone would be close. Marilyn continued to spend all of her time next to Brandon's bed. Weeks and weeks went by. The end of summer was approaching. The Davises tried to talk Marilyn into going on with her life. She didn't want to think about that. Then one evening when she was talking to Brandon like she always did---he opened his eyes.

"Brandon! Brandon!" she exclaimed. "Do you hear me?" Marilyn was so excited. She ran down the hallway to find the nurse on staff. Marilyn and the nurse ran back to the room. The nurse put in a call to notify the doctor.

Brandon's eyes were open, but his eyes wouldn't follow movement. His eyes were blank. It was still an improvement, as far as Marilyn was concerned. If she even slightly entertained the idea of following her parents' advice, this ended it. Marilyn knew in her heart that Brandon was going to get better. Bonnie was there almost as much time as Marilyn. She had to work every day, but she'd relieve Marilyn so Marilyn could follow up with other doctors or attend church with her parents.

One day Marilyn was reading to Brandon from one

of the books that he said he enjoyed. She kept thinking he was changing in some way. Was it the way he looked? What was different, she wondered. Again, as she had done a hundred times before, she held Brandon's hand. "If you can understand me, please squeeze my hand." This time she felt a slight movement. "Yes! Yes! Brandon! I feel it!" she exclaimed. His face was expressionless but she felt movement in his hand. She asked him over and over to move his hand again but there was no response. Did she really feel movement before or did she just imagine it? Did she want it so badly that she imagined it?

With any new change, Marilyn called doctors to see if anything more could be done. She remembered what the doctor told her. He said it was up to God and Brandon. Then Marilyn had a difficult decision to make. She had to find a job and go to work. Since completing her degree, she had been getting various offers, but she turned them all down. She felt she needed to stay with Brandon. Her parents were very gracious in supporting her during this time in her life, but she couldn't expect them to continue supporting her forever. She knew that. If she could secure a job in Slaton, she could still see Brandon at lunch, every evening, and all weekend.

Marilyn accepted a position as a dance and voice instructor at The Fine Arts Academy. If anything, it kept her mind busy during the day. Bonnie was happy to see that Marilyn was doing something positive for herself. Both of them knew that they had to go on with their lives. Sitting and waiting hour after hour, week after week, and month after month was already taking its toll. They were still very devoted to Brandon and would continue to see him every day. The life insurance policy that Brandon's parents had would take care of all of Brandon's medical expenses and Bonnie could live comfortably without working if she didn't want to.

As Marilyn talked to Brandon one evening, she told him all about her students. Marilyn thought that he was actually looking at her. His stare was no longer a blank stare. She knew he was coming back to her. "I see you, Brandon. I see your eyes. You might not be able to say anything yet, but I know you understand. You're coming back, my darling. You're coming back!" she said hugging him with all her might.

What no one knew for sure was that Brandon WAS coming back. Gradually he was able to think and to reason. He couldn't communicate other than slight movement with one hand, but he was starting to figure out what was going on. He knew he was in a hospital setting and nurses came and went throughout the day. Marilyn told him again how he was in a terrible accident, but that he would get better. One day, while his eyes were closed, his nurse came in with a young nurse trainee. Although the nurse whispered to her trainee, Brandon was able to hear what was said.

"Isn't he a handsome fellow?" the nurse said to her trainee. "It was such a terrible thing. He was in a car wreck and sustained severe head and neck injuries. He wasn't expected to live, but he is holding his own. The accident was ten months ago.

I'm afraid he'll never really get any better. Poor man."

Brandon couldn't believe he had been basically 'out' for ten months. He couldn't even remember the accident, and to him, he felt that only a few days had passed. Brandon began feeling trapped inside his body. He could see and hear, but he couldn't talk, and he couldn't move. He couldn't even make sounds. So, all he did was try to remember about his life. *What did I used to do? Who were these people?*

Another two months passed with no more progress being made. Actually, there was no new progress that could be seen outwardly. Inside, Brandon was starting to remember his life before the accident. He remembered Marilyn, but he didn't remember that he was going to propose to her the night after the accident happened. Marilyn and Bonnie continued their vigil in Brandon's room. Sometimes they were there together, and their friendship was great comfort to each of them. Bonnie told Marilyn about Brandon's childhood and growing up with him as a big brother.

Gradually, Brandon remembered everything. He remembered the proposal plan that Bonnie had designed. He remembered the ring. Then he remembered his parents. *Please*, he prayed, *I'm afraid they were with me in the accident. Where are they? I haven't seen them. Please, God, tell me they are alive.* Brandon was only able to talk to God----he couldn't communicate with anyone else.

Weeks went by. Brandon continued to analyze his situation. He realized Marilyn would not go on with her life as long as he was in a facility near her. He loved Marilyn deeply but did not want to ruin her life. He remembered how much she loved dancing. He would never be able to dance with her again. He wanted her to forget about him and start a new life for herself. She needed to be totally free to marry someone who could take her dancing and help her raise the children she always wanted. Somehow, he would have to see that happen. His life, or the rest of his life, would be spent remembering the wonderful times he and Marilyn had together. He loved her more than anything, and if he couldn't give her the life he thought she should have, he didn't want to stand in the way of her being with someone else. He was determined to devise a plan to save her life. It was going to kill him, but he didn't care. His life was pretty much over anyway.

2

As hard as Brandon tried, he couldn't move anything other than his eyes, and he had only very slight movement in one hand. When Marilyn or Bonnie tried to see if Brandon could write when they placed a pencil in his hand, he was unable to do so. He couldn't hold the pencil by himself, and then he couldn't move it even with assistance. Then one day when Marilyn wasn't there, Bonnie figured out that Brandon could answer 'yes' by looking to the right and 'no' by looking to the left. That same night, Bonnie came up with the idea of using an alphabet. If the letters were written large enough, and if she could follow Brandon's eyes, perhaps

Brandon could spell words and communicate. It worked. Bonnie was able to communicate with her brother for the first time since the accident. She knew he could hear and comprehend what others said; he just couldn't respond. Now, maybe he could.

Marilyn missed this new development. She and her students were involved in a musical production, so she was unable to get to the nursing center to see Brandon that evening. Bonnie couldn't wait to tell Marilyn, but Brandon stopped her. When Bonnie told Brandon that she couldn't wait to tell Marilyn, Brandon reacted with a look to the left----'no.'

"No?" Bonnie questioned. "You don't want me to tell Marilyn about how you can communicate?"

Brandon responded with his eyes to indicate 'no' again.

"I don't understand, Brandon. Marilyn loves you more than anything in the world, and she has been by your side almost every day since the accident. I know you can't tell me why----I just don't understand." Again, Brandon responded 'no.' "OK, I won't say anything. I guess I'll figure out why later." Bonnie placed the alphabet card under some papers in the drawer beside his bed.

That night, Bonnie lay in bed thinking about what Brandon wanted and tried to make some sense out of it. Then it suddenly hit her. Knowing her brother like she did, she figured he was somehow going to get Marilyn to go on with her life. Bonnie would ask Brandon about it when she saw him the following day after work.

When Bonnie got to the nursing center after work, Marilyn had already arrived. Marilyn told Brandon all about the musical performance from the night before. Bonnie couldn't say anything to Brandon until they were alone. As the day drew to an end, Bonnie encouraged Marilyn to go home. "Marilyn, you should leave now. I'll give Brandon a sip or two of water and then I'll leave also."

After Marilyn left to go home, Bonnie approached the subject again with Brandon. "Brandon, last night you told me not to tell Marilyn about our communication. I couldn't figure out why you would say that, so I thought about it for hours last night. I finally figured out why. You love Marilyn more than life itself. You think you're not going to be able to lead a normal life, and you want to spare her that kind of life. Is that right, Brandon?" Bonnie questioned with tears in her eyes. Brandon responded with a slight glance to the right, meaning 'yes.'

"Do you know how much she loves you? Are you sure about this? I don't think it matters to her as long as she is with you. Besides, I think you will be fine someday, Brandon. I really do!"

Brandon responded 'yes' again. Then he looked toward the alphabet board as if to tell Bonnie something. Bonnie held it up to Brandon's chest. With movements of his eyes, he spelled.

"T?  Is T right?" Bonnie asked.

Brandon responded, 'Yes.'

"OK, I'll just follow your eyes---go to the next letter if I get it correctly."

Brandon's eyes moved to the "A", then the "K", and then the "E" and Bonnie repeated each letter as he looked at it.  He spelled "M", "E", "A", and "W".  Bonnie repeated each letter.  Brandon then spelled "A" and "Y".  Bonnie wrote the letters down on a piece of napkin as they went.  She wrote: TAKEMEAWAY.  Bonnie looked at the letters for a few seconds and then said, "Take me away?"

Brandon responded, 'Yes' with his eyes.

"Take me away---take me away?  I'm not sure I understand what you mean by that.  I'm sorry, Brandon.  I don't understand, but maybe I can figure it out," Bonnie puzzled.  It was getting late and was time for Bonnie to drive home.  She kept playing Brandon's response over and over in her head.  TAKE ME AWAY.  Does he want to be taken out of the nursing facility?  *No*—she answered herself.  *Brandon knows he has to have the specialized help.*  Bonnie kept thinking and thinking about it.  Finally, she had a thought. *Brandon wants to go away---to some other nursing facility or hospital setting far away, so Marilyn can't visit him daily.  He wants her to get on with her life.  He would give up the person he loves more than life, if he thought doing so would be better for her.* Bonnie thought she broke the code. She would ask Brandon about it tomorrow.

Instead of waiting until after work to see Brandon, Bonnie went during her lunch break. She knew Marilyn wouldn't be there at that time of day. Bonnie hugged her brother then said, "I think I figured it out. You want to make sure Marilyn gets on with her life by going away---far enough away that she can't see you very often. Is that it, Brandon?"

Brandon responded by glancing to the right—'Yes.' It broke Bonnie's heart. She knew Brandon and Marilyn loved each other, but she felt compelled to give Brandon anything he wanted. So much had been taken from him, she couldn't bear to refuse his requests. If she could understand him, she would do exactly as he wanted.

"OK—I'll do anything for you---I'll research facilities up north. I can go with you. I can always get a job and I don't really have anything to keep me .......keep me here." Bonnie caught herself, knowing that Brandon would read between the lines. He looked toward the alphabet board and spelled "M", "O", and then "M" again. Bonnie's heart sank. Tears filled her eyes. She knew exactly what he meant.

"Brandon, Mom and Dad died in the same accident that almost killed you. I'm so very sorry to have to tell you." Bonnie cried. Brandon already knew. When he started healing mentally, he knew the only reason his parents weren't there with him was because they couldn't be.  They never came to his room and no one ever mentioned them.  He already knew.  He just had to ask regardless of how it would hurt Bonnie and hurt him. He had to face it.

Bonnie draped herself across Brandon's bed and wept.  A tear rolled down Brandon's cheek.  All the memories were coming back and sadness overwhelmed him.  Most of the time now, Brandon wished he had died in the accident, too.  Dying would have been much easier than facing everything he had to face now----losing his parents, losing Marilyn, and possibly being an invalid for the rest of his life.

Sensing that Brandon might totally shut down, Bonnie pleaded, "I think I understand what you want. I can tell Marilyn that I have to move you to a special rehabilitation facility, and that I will be with you.  Since I'm a physical therapist, she'll think I know more about the situation and will want to do this as a last effort.  She'll be devastated, but in time, she'll move on with her life."

Brandon moved his eyes to the right—'Yes.'

"I just need time to research facilities and find the very best one for you.  I need to discuss this with your doctors, also." Bonnie was on another mission. After Bonnie conducted her research and talked to several doctors, a facility was located in the Boston area.  Besides being one of the best rehabilitation centers in the United States, it was a long way from Texas--almost 2000 miles to be

234

exact. Bonnie kept Brandon posted as the plans progressed. She dreaded the day she had to tell Marilyn, but she knew it had to happen.

The day finally came. Bonnie had made all the plans to move Brandon. In doing so, she had to make arrangements to sell their house and find a place to live in Boston. When Marilyn arrived in Brandon's room one evening, Bonnie felt it was time to tell her. Marilyn was going to lose Brandon again.

3

"Marilyn, I have something very important to tell you. Brandon's progress has been extremely slow. We don't seem to be making much progress here. There is a rehabilitation facility in the Boston area that has had great results with patients with injuries like Brandon's. It is the best facility in the nation. I want to take Brandon there. I think this may be the key that can unlock Brandon's condition. I feel I must do this!" Bonnie looked and sounded as serious as Marilyn had ever seen her. Bonnie could be quite an actress when she wanted to be.

"Of course!" Marilyn responded. "I want only the best for Brandon. How do we do this?" Bonnie caught the word 'we' in Marilyn's sentence. Bonnie knew breaking away from Marilyn wasn't going to be easy. Marilyn still wanted to be a part of Brandon's life.

"I'll go with him. It will be easy for me to

get a job, probably in the same building Brandon will be in. I'm hoping I can even participate in his rehabilitation program. Besides, you need to stay here and move forward with your life."

Marilyn broke down crying when Bonnie said that. "I'll always love Brandon," Marilyn cried. "I don't know if I can exist without him."

Both Bonnie and Marilyn feared that rehabilitation would produce minimal results, although neither ever spoke about anything other than Brandon getting completely well. They remained positive as a way of keeping their spirits up. Even when Brandon was being wheeled down the hallway to be placed in the car for transporting, Marilyn was still living in her dream that Brandon was going to get better.

Leaning into the van and looking at Brandon, Marilyn felt that he could understand everything that she had to say. "Brandon, I love you more than anything in this world. You make me happier than I have ever been in my life. It doesn't matter that you have been hurt. I want to be with you no matter what kind of life it would be. I don't need anything else if I have you. Do you understand that I don't need anything else? I know in my heart that you are going to get better, but if you never get to that 100% mark, it is still OK with me. I know you are going to get past this, Brandon. Bonnie tells me this new center is the best in the nation. Work hard for all of us. I love you with all my heart and I'll come see you as soon as I can." Marilyn had to turn away from Brandon. She broke down crying, somehow feeling that she was losing him forever.

4

The Richardson Rehabilitation Center for Traumatic Injuries was a most impressive facility--- completely state of the art in every way. Electronic stimulation devices enhanced Brandon's therapy. The slight movement he had in his hand became movement of his whole arm. Everyday Brandon worked hard to move more of his body. No one worked harder than Brandon. In the evenings, Bonnie continued some of his therapy herself. Slowly---very slowly, Brandon was regaining what he had lost.

Marilyn continued to call to check on Brandon's progress. She always called Bonnie since the doctors were never accessible during the hours she could place the call. Bonnie was evasive in her answers to Marilyn. She didn't want to give Marilyn any hope that Brandon would overcome his paralysis although Bonnie saw improvement monthly.

Then one day, something extraordinary happened. Brandon began to speak.

5

Brandon had great difficulty speaking. His voice was labored and was monotone but he could actually talk! Bonnie wanted to tell everyone but was bound by Brandon's wishes. He made it clear to Bonnie that his progress had to be kept secret.

Even his rehabilitation chart had to be carefully labeled as strictly confidential. Only Bonnie had access to his information.

Once when Marilyn couldn't reach Bonnie as she normally did to check on Brandon, she called the center to inquire on his progress. When the attending nurse pulled his file, bold lettering alerted her to the confidentiality of his case. All the worker said was, "Mr. Remington continues to work hard in his rehabilitation efforts." Marilyn took that to mean that no progress had been made. Otherwise, she thought, wouldn't they be anxious to tell her of his progress? She didn't know there was strict confidentiality placed on his file. Sadness filled her heart. So much time had passed, it seemed that Brandon's condition wasn't going to change. Bonnie offered her no hope, either.

When Marilyn contacted Bonnie, Bonnie remained very neutral on Brandon's condition. "Brandon is receiving the best of care. My new job is in the same complex, so I am able to check on him during the day. I stay with him every evening for several hours before going back to my apartment. Marilyn, even if you were here, there is nothing that you could do," Bonnie said. Marilyn's calls became less and less frequent.

Gradually, Brandon's condition improved. He regained movement in his upper torso and arms. He learned how to hold a pencil, comb his hair, and feed himself, and slowly he fought to be normal. While Brandon's life was changing for the better, something happened to also change Marilyn's life.

## Chapter Eleven
## Marilyn's Career Opportunity
## 1937

One evening when Marilyn returned home from her job at the fine arts academy, she received a phone call from the Director of the American Theatrical Production Company. As the man on the other end of the line explained, this company was composed of singers and dancers who travel all over the world performing some of the finest musical productions ever created. Mr. Brent Summers, the director, heard about Marilyn's talents from the professors at the university. Marilyn was impressed with what she heard about his company and appreciated the compliments concerning her talent. This was the type of work that Marilyn had dreamed of doing prior to meeting Brandon. Once she fell in love with him, she put all thoughts of traveling with a production company out of her mind. Marilyn was happy to settle for being a voice and dance instructor as long as she could be with Brandon. That was five years ago!

Marilyn was excited but apprehensive at the same time. She asked Mr. Summers several other questions and then asked if she could have some time to think about his offer. After all, this would mean a major change in Marilyn's life. She decided to talk to Bonnie about it since Brandon was always first and foremost in her mind. Accepting the job would mean that she was moving on with her life. She didn't want to acknowledge that yet. The only positive thing concerning her accepting the job was that she might get to see Brandon more often. With all of the traveling to be done for her job, she'd be in Boston more often.

"Bonnie?" Marilyn asked on the phone. "I need to talk to you. I need to get your advice."

"Sure, what can I do for you?" Bonnie answered.

"I got a call a couple of nights ago from the director of a large production company. He wanted to know if I'd go to work for them. It's something I dreamed of doing before I met Brandon. There's nothing to keep me here any longer. I was thinking that I might get to visit you and Brandon when we tour the Boston area. Maybe I'd be able to see the two of you more often." Marilyn wanted Bonnie's blessing or at least her approval.

"That's great! I think you should do it! You are so talented. You'll be a big hit," Bonnie exclaimed. "You can't let this pass you by! And you're right---I'm sure you'll be traveling up north and you can come see us!" Bonnie didn't know how they would actually handle Marilyn's visiting but they would figure that out when the time came. Brandon still didn't want Marilyn to give up starting a new life. If Marilyn thought Brandon was getting significantly better, she would move to Boston and never leave his side.

Bonnie told Brandon all about Marilyn's call the next day. Brandon, with difficulty, told Bonnie,

"Marilyn… must… do… that. I… want her….
to…. do that." Bonnie understood.

2

After two months of travel, the production company
booked several performances in the Boston area.
Finally, it was Marilyn's chance to see Brandon!
She couldn't wait! Arriving at the rehabilitation
center, Marilyn quickly found the right room.
Brandon was there waiting for Marilyn's arrival, but
he knew he was going to put on the biggest
performance of his life. Marilyn hugged Bonnie but
very quickly turned to Brandon who was strapped in
a chair. Marilyn ran to him, hugged him, and kissed
him on his cheeks. Brandon used every bit of
strength he had to sit motionless. He didn't want
Marilyn to know he could now talk and move his
arms and upper body. If Marilyn knew he was
making this much progress, she would again put her
career behind her, and she would be there for
Brandon. It killed Bonnie to sit there and watch as
Marilyn hugged Brandon, and he didn't respond.
He could have hugged her back---and he
desperately wanted to. He loved Marilyn----he
loved her deeply---so deeply, in fact, that he was
willing to give her up. It hurt Bonnie deeply to see
this drama unfold in front of her eyes. She tried to
hide the tear that trickled down her cheek. She knew
the feelings of love between them.

Marilyn pulled a chair as close to Brandon's wheel
chair as she could get and then told Brandon all
about her new job. He could tell how excited she
was about it. It confirmed that he was making the

right decision although it broke his heart. He lost his parents and now he was losing Marilyn. He remembered someone saying once that to truly love a person meant doing what was best for that person----not what you wanted for yourself. He kept telling himself that—over and over.

"I'll be back again soon," Marilyn told Brandon. "We'll be touring in this area again in a few weeks." She looked at Bonnie with a very sad look in her eyes. She believed Brandon wasn't getting any better. It hurt her so to see Brandon in this state. Brandon had put on the best performance of his life--- and she believed him. He stared straight ahead with a blank look on his face. He wouldn't move. Bonnie remained silent.

Marilyn leaned over and took Brandon in her arms again. She nestled her face into his neck and kissed him on his cheek. A touch of pink lipstick remained near his mouth---a tender reminder of Marilyn's love for him. It was all Brandon could do to not hold her in his arms and kiss her forcefully. He had dreamed of kissing her every day since he could remember. Somedays the thought of kissing her was the only thing that kept him alive. Thinking of their time together that night at her parent's house was way too painful. He couldn't even go there. But he remained strong---for her--- he kept telling himself. Marilyn stood up, looked tearfully at Bonnie and slowly walked out of the room. She wanted to leave before she broke down crying.

When Marilyn walked out of the room, down the hall, and out the front door, she felt like she was walking out of Brandon's life forever. She would come back as soon as she could, but she didn't think Brandon even remembered her. It was so painful to see him and dream of what could have been. Marilyn got in a cab and left for her hotel room. From the back seat of the cab, she glanced back at the hospital. She couldn't believe that the man she loved so deeply was there in that building and maybe unaware that he was even there. The Brandon she loved and couldn't live without was not there. All Marilyn had were memories.

When Marilyn left the room, Bonnie could no longer remain strong. Tears rolled down her cheeks, creating small black lines on her face from her mascara running down her cheek. She quickly wiped her tears away with her hand and then moved closer to Brandon. Brandon glanced over to where she sat---a movement he refused to show when Marilyn was present.

Bonnie walked over to Brandon and knelt down in front of his wheelchair. She looked deeply into his eyes.

"Brandon, I know you have thought through all of this very carefully. I even agree with your decision to some extent, but I still don't see why you can't let her know how much you have progressed. She could still travel if you say that is what you want her to do. She could still be an entertainer. I know she loves you!" Bonnie cried, hoping to help Brandon see another option to what he felt he had to do.

"No, no--- she deserves much, much more."
Brandon managed to say slowly. Then, Bonnie and
one of the nurses helped Brandon get back into his
bed. He turned over, facing the wall, and a tear
silently fell onto his pillow. As sad as it seemed to
Bonnie, she respected her brother's feelings.
Bonnie would do anything in the world for Brandon
and if that were his decision, she would support
him.

3

Sometimes when Brandon was in his physical
therapy, he imagined that he was with Marilyn and
that she was also working out. He'd imagine that
she was next to him, watching his every move as
she did her exercises. It seemed so much easier
when he thought of it that way. He was motivated
to do his best FOR HER. Then he would come
back to reality and his therapy would be grueling.
She was an escape for Brandon. He dreamed about
her every chance he could get.

Brandon came to know the therapists in rehab very
well. One day one of the therapists who was
particularly fond of Brandon asked him if he would
like to venture down to the library near the dining
hall. Brandon had never been in the library before--
he was accustomed to helpers bringing him any
reading materials that he desired. When his
therapist helped him wheel into the library, Brandon
stopped suddenly. On the wall opposite the entry
was a beautiful portrait of Marilyn. It was a large,
framed poster advertising one of Marilyn's dance
performances. Brandon couldn't believe it! His

eyes wouldn't leave the picture. The therapist noticed him staring and asked if he knew her. He couldn't even answer.

"I think this beautiful lady donated some money to our center here and also gave us this beautiful poster some years ago. We had it framed and it's been here since that time! See? It's even autographed!"

There was Marilyn's signature almost hidden in the right corner. Brandon couldn't believe his eyes. The love of his life was in the library all this time and he never knew it! He wondered if Bonnie even knew. He made a mental note to ask her as soon as he could, but for now, he was totally speechless.

"There's something else written here in the corner," the therapist said. "She wrote something else but the frame is partially covering it up! I think it says----here, I can make it out a little bit---'BR, I will always lov----I bet that means 'love you.' I wonder who BR is?" Then the thought came to her. She read Brandon's eyes. Then they both knew. Brandon was speechless but his eyes were very sad.

The next day when Bonnie came to Brandon's room, he mentioned the picture in the library.

"No, I never knew anything about it, Brandon! Funny that I work here, yet I've never been in there. It doesn't surprise me, though. Marilyn was always such a giving person." Brandon didn't tell Bonnie about the note in the corner. Bonnie was curious enough, though, to go to the library and see for herself. She studied the picture from top to bottom, and then her eyes came to rest on the lower right-hand corner. The initials BR stood out clearly. She saw the partial message and knew exactly what it meant. Her heart cried for Brandon and also for Marilyn. She knew that no matter what Marilyn did with the rest of her life, she would always love Brandon-----and she knew it would be the same for him.

4

Marilyn threw herself into her work. Since she resolved herself to the fact that she would never have a life with Brandon, she didn't care about how much she traveled. She didn't care how grueling her life would be. She spent as much time as she could with her parents and they frequently met her at her performances. They were so proud of Marilyn for her accomplishments but their hearts broke because of the life that had been stolen from her. Marilyn became a very successful performer, traveling all over the world. Her life was no life. She woke up in hotel rooms and frequently forgot where she was. In a way, it was an escape for her. If she remained extremely busy, she wouldn't have much time to think about a home or children, especially if she couldn't even remember what city she was in or where she would spend her next night.

Marilyn was famous. She was loved by everyone, yet she experienced no love for herself. She led a lonely, lonely existence.

Brandon continued to make progress in his healing

efforts. With excellent physical therapy provided during the day, and additional therapy provided in the evenings by Bonnie, Brandon was able to stand with the aid of a special brace. His arms got stronger, and some motion came back to his hands and fingers. The speech pathologist worked diligently---and Brandon worked diligently to improve his speech. Soon he could speak more fluently, yet it was still laborious. He was also determined to walk again. He knew it was just a matter of time. Brandon had progressed to the point where he could leave the rehabilitation center. He moved into Bonnie's apartment and mostly got around in a wheelchair. He continued physical therapy and improved to the point where he could get around with the help of a walker.

The day finally arrived when Brandon wanted to walk outside. With Bonnie's help, Brandon made it out of the door and onto the front sidewalk. He couldn't remember the last time he actually stood on a sidewalk outside to let the sunshine stream down on him. He took a few steps and then stopped again. He looked at the trees and marveled at their beauty. He saw the trees from the windows in the apartment, but he hadn't really looked at them. Not really. His mind was on other things. Now he could see the trees----and see the flowers---and the birds---and the clouds in the sky. For the first time since his accident, Brandon felt like he could really live again. He knew he was getting better and felt he could make something out of the rest of his life.

No matter how Brandon tried to move on with his life, he never lived one day without thinking about

Marilyn, even if only for a brief moment. He never doubted that he had done the right thing in allowing Marilyn to move forward with her career. She was doing extremely well and had become one of the most popular performers across the country. Brandon was so proud of her.

Sometimes when Brandon had difficulty sleeping at night, he dreamed about what kind of life they could have had together if the accident hadn't happened. He replayed his plans for the marriage proposal over and over in his head. He could see her vividly, reacting to his proposal, as he knew she probably would. Some nights, his dreams took him to the actual wedding ceremony. Brandon could feel himself standing by the altar, waiting for Marilyn and her father to appear at the back entrance---for the walk down the aisle.

In his dream, she was absolutely stunning and her eyes were fixed on Brandon. He saw his parents sitting on the first pew, grinning from ear to ear. Occasionally, his mother would dab her eyes with her handkerchief, after shedding tears of happiness. Brandon relived what he felt had been taken from him, and he learned to do it well. He lived the action and felt the sensations. He could smell the flowers and could hear the organ music. Thinking and dreaming about Marilyn allowed him to connect to her. If that is all he would ever have of her, he would accept it. At least he would have his dreams.

In the back of Bonnie's mind, though, she wondered if somehow Brandon and Marilyn could still get together. Marilyn continued to call but only seldom now and she never mentioned anything about her life. Bonnie abided by Brandon's wishes and never offered information to Marilyn. Finally, the calls came few and far between. It was just too sad for Marilyn.

Brandon kept up with Marilyn's career by reading the reviews in the newspapers. One day when Bonnie returned home from work, Brandon handed her a note he had written: *What would you think about driving into New York for the weekend? Marilyn is performing at the Kennedy Theatre Saturday night. I would like to see her perform.* His writing was barely legible, but he kept trying and it was improving.

Bonnie was shocked! Brandon never wanted to go anywhere! This was definitely a change for Brandon. Bonnie felt happy, but she also felt sad. She knew Brandon was still in love with Marilyn, and she didn't know what kind of emotional pain he would endure by seeing her on stage.

"Are you sure you want to do this, Brandon?" Bonnie asked as she wheeled Brandon to the kitchen table. "This might be pretty draining on you physically. Are you up to it?"

"Yes---yes, I think I can," Brandon replied

slowly.

"Then that is exactly what we're going to do!" Bonnie answered cheerfully. "Let's drive over tomorrow morning, so we can get checked into the hotel in time to rest before we have to get ready for the show. Just getting out of the car and into the performance hall will be more than you are used to, but you'll be fine."

Brandon knew it would be difficult, but he didn't care. He wanted to see Marilyn, and nothing was going to keep him from doing just that.

## Chapter Twelve
## Marilyn's Performance

The lobby of the Kennedy Theatre was filling up quickly. The performance started at 8:00 pm sharp, and everyone wanted to arrive early enough to find seats. People milled around, visiting with friends, and acquaintances they knew. Bonnie pulled up to the front entrance, helped Brandon out of the car, and then turned it over to the valet. While he waited for her, he looked around at the buildings and cars and people scurrying around crazily. He didn't feel comfortable at all, and his energy was already diminishing. Bonnie helped Brandon through the front door, and he maneuvered cautiously with his walker.

"Would you stand here for just a minute?" Bonnie asked, "I just need to go to the ladies' room. I'll be right back. Will you be OK?" Brandon nodded affirmatively.

Brandon stood near the front door, looking very handsome in his dark suit and burgundy tie. Meanwhile, Marilyn had a few minutes before the performance and wanted to leave a message at the front door, so she wove her way through the crowd to get to the front of the lobby. From across the lobby, she caught a glimpse of Brandon but told herself that it couldn't be! She couldn't see the walker since so many people were blocking the view. For a split second her heart fluttered. She convinced herself that it couldn't be Brandon. *Why did I think that?*

"Miss Davis! Miss Davis!" An admiring fan stopped her along the way to congratulate her on an earlier performance. "I just wanted to tell you that we saw your performance last week in Chicago. It was absolutely wonderful and you were the best of the best! My husband and I are here tonight just because of you!" the silver-haired lady exclaimed smiling brightly.

"Oh! Thank you so very much! Dancing is my passion, of course, but I couldn't do this without wonderful people like you coming to see me! I really appreciate each and every one of you!" Marilyn responded politely but was driven to get to the front door to find the man who looked like Brandon. Her heart was pounding. She had a feeling of urgency.

Meanwhile, Bonnie returned to Brandon and helped him through the crowd. They wanted to find their seats. Marilyn looked to the exact place where she thought she had seen Brandon standing. She looked around rather frantically but couldn't see anyone who resembled him. *It couldn't possibly be Brandon,* Marilyn thought----*so why am I looking so hard for him?* She turned and walked away.

2

The performance was spectacular. Never had a production been filled with such beautiful costumes and set designs. The singers and dancers were true professionals, but Marilyn stood out among them all. Having already secured a great reputation and quite a following of fans, Marilyn entered onto the stage and was met with a huge roar of applause from the audience. Bonnie glanced at Brandon to see how he was reacting. He smiled. His eyes said that he was more in love with Marilyn than ever---- and Bonnie knew that.

During one of Marilyn's dramatic songs, she scanned the audience as she had always done. It was very difficult to see faces with the stage lights shining in her eyes, but sometimes she could make out facial features. As she scanned to the back of the audience, she saw the man who she thought looked like Brandon. She kept singing, but it was obvious that her eyes were transfixed on one point. Bonnie certainly noticed it, so Brandon probably did, too. When her song was finished, Marilyn exited the stage quickly. Then, Marilyn tried to find the man from behind the curtain. She couldn't see him. *Why am I looking?* She asked herself. *It couldn't possibly be Brandon! I'm sure it was just someone who looked like Brandon.*

With a few minutes left in the last act, Brandon told Bonnie, "Let's go now."

"Yes," Bonnie replied, "Let's get out of here before the end and there is a mass exodus."

Bonnie thought Brandon wanted to get out ahead of the crowd because of his walker. Brandon really wanted to get out before Marilyn had a chance to find him. He was right. As soon as the final curtain fell, Marilyn ran down the aisle to where she thought she had seen him. He was already gone.

The next day, Marilyn couldn't help but call Bonnie to inquire, "Bonnie, I could have sworn that I saw Brandon last night at my performance in New York. Am I crazy or what?"

Bonnie's heart sank but she pulled herself together to say, "Really? You thought you saw him? Well, I think Brandon is probably at every production you are in ----in your heart. He always loved your singing and dancing."

"Yes, he is always in my heart," Marilyn replied sadly, feeling like she had gotten her answer. Marilyn kept playing the evening before over and over in her mind. She replayed seeing Brandon in the lobby and then again in the audience. *Was I just dreaming?* she asked herself. She wanted to dream that he was really there. She wanted her dream to be true.

## Chapter Thirteen
### Brandon's Recovery

Brandon kept track of Marilyn and kept a box full of newspaper clippings that reviewed her performances. He continued physical therapy to the point where he only needed a cane for walking. His speech improved tremendously, although it still remained slower than normal. He reviewed his accounting manuals and regained his confidence in accounting practices. Finally, after many years of rehabilitation and hard work, Brandon regained his mobility and was able to secure a job. Brandon didn't have to work---there was plenty of insurance money to last the rest of his life---but he needed to work to get his mind off Marilyn. His speech was fine.

One evening after dinner Bonnie asked, "Brandon, now that you are doing so well, why don't we contact Marilyn? I know she would want to hear from you."

"No, Marilyn is at the peak of her career. She wouldn't give that up now, but I don't want her to even be faced with the decision. I love her now as much as I ever have, but I can't put her in that position. Besides, she couldn't possibly feel the same about me after all these years. It's been over five years," Brandon answered. "Besides, what could I offer her now? Come be with me and give up your exciting, world-famous career? Or, keep your career but come see me every other month or so? I can't even dance with her, and she loves dancing so much. No, she has moved on with her life, and I must accept that."

Even though Brandon verbalized that he wouldn't contact Marilyn, the idea kept going through his head. Maybe someday, he thought---maybe someday. Another year passed by. Then when Brandon found the latest review for another performance Marilyn had been in, he noticed a picture. The picture showed Marilyn with a nice-looking gentleman by her side. The caption read: Miss Marilyn Davis accepts engagement ring from director Charles Summers. Brandon's heart sank. He felt himself being pulled down into a deep, deep depression. He knew someday this would probably happen, but he never believed it would have such an effect on him. *Isn't this what I wanted for her? Yes*---but even knowing this, it hurt him deeply. He loved Marilyn so much and he had for so many years.

Charles was the director of the company that Marilyn worked for after Brandon had his accident. Brandon assumed they had fallen in love and were getting married. He wanted the very best for Marilyn, but he was still very much in love with her.

He remembered back to the day he saw Marilyn's picture with Mark, the attorney her father had introduced her to one day in his office. That picture made the paper, also. Brandon took care of that situation. *I can't and won't do anything about this situation*, he thought. Instead of being happy-- after all, his plan for her worked---he was deeply depressed. He was forced to face the reality of losing her forever. He cut the picture and article out of the paper as he had done for the past few years. He put it in the same box with all of the other articles. The only difference, he thought, was that he would end it there. He would no longer follow her career. It was time to put that part of his life away. Bonnie saw the picture lying on the kitchen table. She never mentioned anything about it to Brandon---and he never mentioned it either. Bonnie's hope that Brandon and Marilyn would someday get together ended with that picture.

2

Charles gave Marilyn a beautiful engagement ring, just like the picture showed. What the picture didn't show was Marilyn's feelings about getting it.

"Marilyn," Charles said after he presented her with the ring. "I really love you, and I want us to spend the rest of our lives together."

"Charles, you are a wonderful man. You gave me an opportunity to do what I have always wanted to do. You have been a great mentor, and I respect you greatly. I'm just afraid that I can't be what you want me to be. When Brandon almost died in that accident, a part of me died. I've never been able to get over him. I thought if I threw myself into my career, that I'd quit thinking so much about him, but it never happened."

"I know you loved him, but you were so young. He was a wonderful man, but he's not the man you fell in love with now. His accident changed all of that." Charles pleaded.

"I know---I know. But for some reason, I continue to think about him all the time. Could you marry me knowing that? Could you?" Marilyn asked.

"Yes, I can. I know that we can have a beautiful life together. We can travel all over the world. You love singing and dancing----this is your life. Being together can only make all of that better."

Marilyn didn't have butterflies in her stomach when she looked at Charles the way she remembered when she looked at Brandon. She thought she would probably never have those feelings again. *I'm not getting any younger,* she thought to herself. *Since I can't have the life with Brandon that I so hoped to have, then I guess this is the next best thing.*

## Chapter Fourteen
## Marilyn Returns Home
## August 1964

Over twenty years had gone by. Marilyn married
Charles Summers, and they continued to work in
the musical production business. Their life together
was hard--- traveling all over the world. The couple
never had children. After almost 20 years of
marriage, Marilyn and Charles divorced amicably.
She could no longer live the entertainer's life and
wanted to move back to her hometown of Slaton.
Besides, her parents were getting older, and she
needed to be closer to them during this time of their
lives. Charles didn't want Marilyn to leave, but he
understood her desire to put down roots. He told
her he would always be there for her if she ever
needed him----for anything.

Marilyn bought the little cottage on Summersong
Lane. It was the perfect place for her. She resumed
teaching again on a limited basis and enjoyed her
retirement. She loved that little house. For the next
few years, Marilyn enjoyed the relaxed life that
Slaton had to offer. At first it was bitter sweet.
Returning to Slaton after so many years rekindled
many, many memories---many wonderful--- but
many sad. The park and the creek that Marilyn and
Brandon loved to visit was still there and remained
pretty much the same. She remembered the giant
goldfish. Wildflowers still grew around town and
Marilyn remembered that those wildflowers were

Brandon's floral shops. The flower flattened in the book after their first date was just a memory. Maudie's, the little tearoom where Marilyn first met Brandon had been gone for quite some time, also. She remembered the laughter. More and more, Marilyn used the memories to comfort her as she made her life in the little house.

Sometimes, when Marilyn felt like dancing, she put a record on the phonograph and she danced around the living-room floor. She seemed to glide with the beat of the music. More times than she could remember, she imagined Brandon dancing with her. She remembered the night they won the dance contest. That had been over 35 years ago when she was only 20 years old. Where had all of the years gone? What would her life had been like if Brandon had not had his accident? She could only dream.

## Chapter Fifteen
## Brandon Returns Home
## 1968

Brandon retired from his accounting position and Bonnie wanted a change, also. They talked more and more about returning to Slaton where the lifestyle was slower and more relaxed. Neither of them had a clue that Marilyn had moved back to Slaton many years earlier. After Marilyn married, Brandon quit following her career. In fact, he wanted to close that chapter of his life book. It was too painful. He continued to dream about the good times they had---but that is all they were---dreams.

Brandon and Bonnie found a house a few blocks from the house they grew up in. It was comforting to be back home. In no time at all, they became involved in the community and church activities. In fact, the local paper ran a little article about their 'homecoming.' It chronicled Brandon's accident, and his recovery. The town's community star was returning home! Brandon's picture was in the paper and he looked dashing---absolutely dashing.

2

One morning, bright and early, Marilyn walked in her backyard garden carrying her pruning shears. She had several rosebushes growing against the back fence that really needed a good clipping. She gathered a beautiful bouquet of roses of all different colors---red, yellow, white, pink, and peach----and then carefully pruned off the dead buds. She couldn't help but think of the first time when she walked with Brandon in the park. She smiled when she thought of him picking little wildflowers and placing them in her hair. Marilyn felt blessed that she had such good memories of their time together. What wonderful memories were made in those few, short months. Brandon and Marilyn were together only seven months before the tragic accident and much of that time, Marilyn was away at school. She still felt blessed that she had so many wonderful memories to cling to at this stage of her life.

Marilyn enjoyed reading the local paper. It was interesting to find out who was getting married, who had died, and what school had won the Blue Ribbon of Excellence Award from the state. Imagine her surprise -----no, imagine her shock when she saw Brandon's picture in the paper. Her heart started fluttering just like it used to do. She read the name over and over. Brandon Remington? Brandon Remington? Is it really him? Yes! It looks like him! She read the article at least three times---reading it, then standing up, walking around the table, sitting to read it again, over and over. What was she going to do? The article said nothing about Brandon being married. She read it again just to make sure. She had to see him. She couldn't wait.

3

Marilyn called the newspaper and got Brandon's address. After putting on her prettiest dress and combing her hair just right, she drove to the address she had written on a little slip of paper. She walked up to the front door and knocked. Her heart was pounding; she was short of breath. After what seemed like an eternity, Brandon opened the door. When Brandon saw Marilyn, he saw the most beautiful woman in the whole world. He was completely in shock. Before he could say one word, Marilyn threw her arms around him. He also held her in his arms tightly. Neither one of them said a word. Brandon didn't want to let her go. Neither did Marilyn. Finally, they pulled back from each other but remained holding hands.

"Oh, Marilyn, you are so beautiful. You are as beautiful now as you were when I first met you. Are you still performing?" Brandon asked lovingly.

"Heavens no! I gave that up years ago. I moved back here after my divorce. I give a few dance lessons from time to time. I'm enjoying my retirement here. Thank goodness that I read the paper this morning. I saw your picture!" Marilyn said. "But----when----how----why didn't??..."

"There are a lot of questions to answer, I know," Brandon said as he hugged her once again. Brandon invited her inside to sit in the living room. They talked and talked and talked. After all, they had many years of catching up to do. They laughed as much as they once did. All of the feelings surfaced. They had never been extinguished; they were only tucked away, somewhere deep in their hearts. They talked late into the night, leaving the house only to have dinner. Marilyn and Brandon drove over to her little house on Summersong Lane so he could see where she had spent the last few years of her life. He loved it.

As the grandfather clock struck midnight, Brandon held Marilyn in his arms and kissed her passionately. "I'm not going to let you get away this time," Brandon said.

"And I am not going to let you get away either--ever," Marilyn said with conviction.

They talked about Marilyn's career and all of the traveling that she had done over the years. Very little was said about the accident that almost killed Brandon. Marilyn felt it was just too sad, and she had always felt guilty for not staying next to Brandon's side although she was right there on a daily basis for months and months. Brandon didn't discuss his rehabilitation because he didn't want her to know that he knew he was getting better back in those days. All of this would be discussed someday, but not until it was the right time.

Brandon left Marilyn standing at the front door of her home. He felt happier than he had been since before the accident. As far as he was concerned, he was going to follow the same plan he and Bonnie put together when Marilyn was 21 and he was 27.

The next morning, Brandon told Bonnie all about the surprise. Bonnie missed everything since she was babysitting until very late with her neighbor's child. She would have given anything to see their reunion.

"Bonnie, what ever happened to the engagement ring I bought for Marilyn?" Brandon asked. Bonnie knew that Brandon had never asked about the ring—not once in all these years. But Bonnie had it and she kept it all this time, safe and secure in her safety deposit box at the bank.

"I have it for you. Are you telling me that I might *finally* get a sister-in-law?" Bonnie asked with tears streaming down her face. "Oh, Brandon! This is wonderful!"

"Bonnie---I made the decision that I thought I had to make many years ago. I loved Marilyn so much then that I had to do what I thought was best for her. Maybe I made a horrible mistake. Maybe I should have done things differently but there's no use in talking about that now. That time is gone forever. What I do know now, is that I still love Marilyn---perhaps more now than ever before. I'm not going to let her be anywhere except with me. I have to make up for all of the things I was never able to do for her over these many years. I'll pray that God will let me be the perfect husband for her now."

Brandon took his wallet out of his pocket and pulled out a small, yellow piece of paper. It was so old that it was crumbling on the edges. It was the note Bonnie had written for Brandon to remind him of the steps he was supposed to take for proposing to Marilyn over 40 years ago. Bonnie cried when she saw it.

"Do I still follow this?" Brandon asked as

his voice started to crack. He looked at Bonnie and then smiled like he had never smiled before.

"I'll get the ring right now. You think of what to do," Bonnie said, wiping the tears from her eyes. Bonnie left and Brandon called Marilyn on the phone. "Please say you will go with me to the park down by the creek," Brandon said convincingly.

"Of course, I'll go!" Marilyn cried. "I thought you would never ask."

As soon as Bonnie got back with the ring, Brandon left. He drove over to Marilyn's house, but they decided to walk the short distance to the park. It was as if not one day had passed since their last visit to the park. It was obvious they were both in love with each other---as much as before.

"Do you think we'll see the giant goldfish?" Bonnie asked with a twinkle in her eye.

"Oh! I'm sure we will!" Brandon answered. "He might be in a wheelchair but he will be there!" They laughed and held each other tightly.

4

It was getting late; the sun was going down behind the trees. No one was around. Brandon led Marilyn over to the picnic table and seated her there.

"Marilyn, my darling. I have a lot to say so please be patient with me." He paused and then cleared his throat. "I fell totally in love with you over 40 years ago. Bonnie and I carefully planned out the day that I would ask you to marry me. The ring was engraved with two dates---the first, May 27, 1932, the date that we first met and the second, December 13, 1932 ---the second was the date we were to become engaged." When Marilyn heard that tears started streaming down her face. Brandon continued, "The accident happened the night before and my whole life changed. When I finally realized what had happened and what shape I was in, I made the decision to let you go. I loved you more than anything in the whole world, but I didn't want to be a weight around your neck. I wanted you to finally realize your dream of performing around the world. That's why we couldn't keep in touch with you on my progress----I felt I had to let you go if I really loved you---and I did---I do. Although I let you go, I never ever stopped loving you. I kept track of you through newspaper articles and magazine articles. It wasn't until you married that I knew I had to stop following your career. Even then, not a single day went by without my thinking about you. If the only way I could have you would be in my dreams, then I would take that. When you appeared at my door yesterday, it was like you never left. It was like nothing had changed. I don't ever want you to leave me. I love you."

Tears were streaming down Marilyn's face. She was speechless. Then Brandon set his cane aside and sat down next to Marilyn on the park bench. He pulled the ring out of his pocket.

"Marilyn, this is the ring. This is the exact ring I had for you in 1932. I love you. Will you please marry me?"

Marilyn threw her arms around Brandon. "Yes---yes---yes!" she cried through her sobs. Brandon slipped the ring on her finger. "It's beautiful!" she said softly. They walked back to her house, and Brandon showed her the slip of paper he had been carrying since 1932. She cried again, but she was the happiest person in the entire world.

The next day, Brandon and Marilyn visited her parents and told them everything. They couldn't have been happier for the couple.

"If it is OK with you," Brandon said, "We're going to have a very short engagement. We'd like to get married this weekend, with your blessing." Brandon and Marilyn grinned from ear to ear.

Brandon knew at their age it wasn't necessary to ask her parents, but he wanted to do it anyway.

They were married by the justice of the peace down at the courthouse. Only Marilyn's parents and Bonnie were present. Then Brandon moved in with Marilyn to start their life together. There was never a happier couple on the face of the Earth. They loved each other's company so much, they didn't need to venture outside of the home very often. Brandon loved watching Marilyn dance around the living room. She loved watching him putter in the backyard, trimming his beloved rose bushes. He had one particular favorite---a beautiful, pink hybrid.  They ventured out to church on Sunday and Brandon reminded Marilyn of the time she surprised him with a solo one Sunday morning.

5

On their first Valentine's Day together, Marilyn cooked Brandon a special dinner.  She prepared all of his favorite things----meat loaf, mashed potatoes with gravy, broccoli, and yellow squash.  Brandon presented her with a beautiful, red-satin, heart-shaped box of candy.  The top was almost completely covered with deep, red velvet roses.

"I've never seen such a beautiful Valentine box!  I must keep it forever!" Marilyn was overwhelmed with emotion.

"We never celebrated Valentine's Day---this is our very first.  That's why it is so special," Brandon explained.  "We met that summer, spent Thanksgiving together and almost made it to Christmas but we never had a Valentine's Day together."

They ate the candy, only a piece or two a day, until the box was completely empty.  Marilyn then took the box and placed it on top of the armoire in her bedroom.  Occasionally, she would remove it, dust it off, and put it back in its place.  From the day that Brandon and Marilyn got back together, Marilyn kept a diary of their life together.  She began with a preface of what had happened to them many years ago and how they finally got back together---41 years later.  Some people would say it was a beautiful love story with true-to-life characters. Marilyn treasured what she wrote and read special excerpts to Brandon often in the evenings.

## Chapter Sixteen
## Marilyn's Diary

*August 13, 1968*

*It doesn't matter what happened over the past 40 years. It only matters what is happening now. Brandon moved into my house today---now it is 'ours.' I cleared out a closet in the bedroom, three drawers in the chest, and one side of the bathroom vanity. He said he felt at home immediately. He absolutely loves the backyard----I think it is going to be his favorite place. He loves roses, so I have relinquished the responsibility of the roses to him. He gets along very well with his cane and threatens to use it on me if I 'get out of line.' I realized once Brandon came back into my life that I have missed out on 40 years of laughter. We have a lot of catching up to do.*

*August 27, 1968*

*Today Brandon showed me the box of newspaper and magazine clippings that he kept about my career. It was so much fun seeing me at such a young age. Brandon is determined to make a scrapbook, and he said he will work on it, a little each day. He showed me the picture he cut out of Charles giving me the engagement ring. That's when he quit collecting articles. I explained to Brandon why I married Charles. None of that matters anymore. We are so happy together.*

*Bonnie came over for dinner tonight. I think she may be funnier than Brandon! What a great time we had!*

*September 5, 1969*

*Today we went to the cemetery to place flowers on Brandon's parents' graves. They were such wonderful people. It's so sad that they weren't alive to see us get married. At least before they died in the accident, they knew we were going to get married. I think they are looking down on us and joining in on our happiness.*

*October 20, 1970*

*Brandon and I bought a swing for the backyard. How delightful to sit and swing among beautiful roses and geraniums! We talked about what our lives would have been like if the accident hadn't happened. It was fun to dream---it really wasn't sad---it was fun to imagine. The only regret, that both of us have now, is that we never had children to share our last years with.*

*November 23,1972*

*It snowed last night! It is absolutely beautiful here. A white blanket of snow covers our yard and our mountain has a beautiful white cap. Brandon and I sat on the window seat, enjoying our morning coffee and admired the white wonderland. I could sit here with Brandon for the rest of my life. I thank God every day that we are together.*

273

*December 20, 1972*

*Bonnie has a beau. She met Randell several years ago, but now they are quite serious. I think they'll get married soon. I'll never forget how she helped Brandon when he was injured. She is a wonderful sister and a wonderful sister-in-law.*

*January 30, 1973*

*We bought carpet for the living room floor. The hardwood floor is scratched up pretty badly. It would take complete refinishing to look presentable, so we decided to buy carpet. I don't do much dancing anymore, anyway. Brandon said we could lie in front of the fireplace on the carpet when it is really cold. We laughed that it would be fun if we could get back up off the floor. Our joints are pretty stiff these days.*

*Brandon told me a really funny joke today. I have to write it down pretty fast since I can never remember jokes! I am the worst!*

*OK—Here it goes----*
*A man and his wife went to the mall to shop for Christmas presents. Their list was long and they had a lot of shopping to do. When the wife came out of the store and looked around for her husband, he was gone! Irritated, she paged him and waited for his return call. "Where have you been! I have been looking for you for almost an hour! You know we have so much shopping to do and I don't want to be here until midnight!"*

*"Well," her husband answered. "You know that jewelry store that we walked into about six months ago?"*

*"Yes!" she answered excitedly.*

*"Remember that beautiful necklace that you wanted and I told you we couldn't buy it then but we would buy it someday?"*

*"Yes! Yes!" she was getting more excited by the minute.*

*"Well, I am at the bar next door to that store."*

*I thought that was hilarious. Brandon knows I am a good audience for his jokes.*

*June 13, 1964*

*Today was a very special day. Brandon brought me a carved-stone vase. It is so beautiful but SO heavy. The perfect place for it is on top of the brick pillar at the end of the fence near the driveway, but I was afraid if it fell, it could kill someone. Today Brandon cemented the stone vase to the top of the pillar. To show how much I love him, I will keep fresh flowers in the case to greet him when he walks down the driveway.*

*October 5, 1964*

*Brandon bought a plane today.  Yes---you read it right---an airplane.  He loves to fly.  He said it gives him a special freedom that can't be explained. In the sky, he doesn't need his cane, and he can go as fast as he wants!  I'm really happy for him.  I don't like flying, so we've decided that he can fly and I will crochet and knit.*

*October 7, 1970*

*You should see Brandon's pink rose bush!  I think it must have thirty roses on it.  They are so beautiful. If he can keep them blooming until fair time, he can enter one in the competition.  He trims on the bush everyday-----except in the winter!*

*February 8, 1975*

*I had a little dizzy spell today.   Brandon is making me go to Dr. McNutt. It's probably nothing.  I am really doing pretty well for my age, especially now that we are walking every day.  We bundle up in our heavy coats and scarves and walk down the street and back.  The only time we miss our walk is if it is icy.  Brandon said he doesn't want to have to take care of me if I fall and break my hip.*

*February 19, 1975*

*The doctor wanted to run more tests, so I'm scheduled for another x-ray next week.  The spells are getting a little worse. Sometimes I lose my balance and bump into the door frame.  I look like*

276

*I'm drunk. Brandon asked me if I was a closet drinker and just hadn't told him about my alcohol problem.*

## Chapter Seventeen
## Marilyn's Illness

Brandon took Marilyn to the clinic for additional testing. Their follow-up appointment was that Friday. After shaking hands with Dr. Durley and Dr. McNutt, Brandon and Marilyn sat in the leather chairs pulled up to the front of the desk.

"Marilyn, the reason you've had some difficulty with dizziness and balance is that there is a small growth---a small tumor—in that region of your brain. We'll need to do a biopsy to determine if it is malignant---many of them aren't---and how we should proceed." Dr. Durley tried to be as positive as he could be in light of the fact that it was bad news.

"Do you think you can just take it out?" Marilyn asked.

"I won't know that quite yet. I'm calling in a brain specialist to consult on this. I want to do the very best thing for you," he answered.

Brandon was numb. He never dreamed she had a serious problem. He wanted to back up the time and erase this scene from his mind. Driving home, Brandon acted as positive as he could.

"You'll be fine, Marilyn. Remember, I had a severe brain injury and nearly died, yet I'm here today! The world of medicine can do some pretty amazing things."

"Oh, I know. I feel in my heart that I will be fine. It's just that our life is so wonderful. I don't want anything to mess that up," Marilyn answered.

*March 4, 1976*

*The test results showed a small tumor in my brain. I'm hoping they can operate and take it out. We will hear sometime next week.*

Brandon took Marilyn in for more tests and another consultation when the results were ready. Dr. Durley introduced Dr. Brannigan to the anxious couple.

"This is Dr. Brannigan. He is the finest brain specialist you'll find anywhere."

Prior to this meeting, Brandon talked to Dr. Brannigan and Dr. Durley when the lab results were available without Marilyn knowing about it. When Brandon learned that the tumor was malignant and fast growing, he insisted that the doctors not tell Marilyn. Brandon didn't want her to know anything other than it was a small tumor that the doctors would remove.

When they met with the doctors, Dr. Durley said, "Marilyn, your tumor is small, but I know it's giving you some trouble. If you approve, Dr. Brannigan will do surgery to remove as much as he can. Hopefully, it is contained and hasn't spread to other parts of the brain. I'll be able to tell more after surgery.

Brandon and Marilyn asked several more questions and decided to go forward with the surgery. Marilyn hadn't told Brandon, but she was losing some of her sight and her ability to smell. When Brandon held one of his beloved roses up to Marilyn's nose to smell the perfume, she couldn't smell anything---but she didn't tell him.

"Beautiful---just beautiful!" she replied without letting on that she couldn't smell anything. She began losing her appetite and was losing weight fast.

*March 9, 1976*

*I go in the hospital for surgery tomorrow. If for some reason I don't survive-----whoever finds this---please tell Brandon that I love him more than anything in the whole world. If I die, I will come back for him someday. Until then, I will wait for him and will be with him in his heart.*

Brandon nervously waited for the surgery to be over. He sat in the waiting room with Bonnie by his side. He couldn't think about anything else but Marilyn. He knew she was in the operating room and was with the best surgical team anywhere. They were real experts. Brandon sat reliving the events of his life, one by one. Funny how life is, he thought. *There are happy times and there are sad times. It doesn't matter if you've tried to live your life in the right way, tragic things can still happen to you. When you are at your happiest, terrible things can happen. You just need to live each day as if it is your last. If you love someone, you must enjoy that person every single day. If you love to dance, you should dance a little every day. If you like to laugh, laugh a little every day.*

He wondered if he did the right thing when he let Marilyn go away when he was in Boston in rehabilitation. He did what he did so that her life could be fulfilled. *But was it?* She convinced him that it wasn't. He realized as he sat in the waiting room that he should have handled things differently in Boston. They should have been together all those years----it was too late to think about what could have been. He needed to be thankful for the 18 years he had with Marilyn so far. Brandon was convinced that Marilyn would not get better---only worse. He didn't even need the doctors to tell him. He already knew. Bonnie tried to talk to him to help the time pass but gave up. She saw that he was in deep thought. She decided to sit quietly beside him, ready to talk if he wanted to. Hours passed.

"Bonnie, we've been through a lot together, haven't we?" Brandon said.

"Yes, we have. Both good and bad."

"There are things I would change if I could live my life over."

"There's not a single person who would not change something about his life. That's normal."

"But you were right, Bonnie. You were right when we were in Boston. If I had just listened

281

to you."

"I just knew how much Marilyn loved you and I knew how much you loved her."

I need to make Marilyn as happy as I possibly can for the rest of her life. That's exactly what I'm going to do."

"You two have had a wonderful life for the past 18 years. You've had more happiness in those years than most people have in an entire lifetime. So, in a way, you've been blessed more than most."

"Leave it up to you to be positive--- you always are." Brandon hugged his sister. She was there for him---always.

The door to the waiting room opened and the doctor walked toward Brandon. He and Brandon walked into a small conference room together with Bonnie following closely behind. As the doctor adjusted his glasses, somewhat nervously, he said, "Brandon, Marilyn did well through the surgery. She's in the recovery room now, and you'll get to see her once she is back in her regular room." The doctor looked at Brandon without smiling. Brandon knew something wasn't right.

"Is she going to be OK, then, doctor?" Brandon asked anxiously.

With a frown on his face and his arm reaching onto Brandon's shoulder, the doctor said, "No, Brandon, she's not. The tumor has spread and has grown rapidly. I removed all that I could, but most of it is inoperable. I'm sorry. We just need to keep her as comfortable as possible. Her brain will gradually start shutting down. I wish there was something more I could do."

Brandon couldn't believe what he was hearing. He couldn't accept it. He lost Marilyn before because of his accident, and now he was losing her when their life seemed so perfect.

"Dr. Brannigan," Brandon said with a very serious tone. "We mustn't tell Marilyn. We have to give her hope, even if there isn't any. Let me handle this."

"I'll do anything you want. Just let me know."

When Marilyn woke up from her surgery, Brandon was right at her side. He leaned over and kissed her. She was still very groggy but smiled when she saw him.

"How did I do?" she asked him.

"You did great! Just great! We are so lucky to have such a wonderful surgeon. You'll be up dancing in no time at all," Brandon said in a performance all of his own. Marilyn felt comforted by his response.

In a few days, Marilyn was strong enough to go home. When she was still dizzy, Brandon told her that was to be expected. When she had difficulty with her balance, Brandon told her that was to be expected. "Healing takes a long time, darling. You have to be patient!" He hugged her tightly.

Marilyn respected what Brandon had to say, but she noticed she really wasn't getting any better. She didn't tell him that, however. There were subtle changes that Marilyn noticed but didn't tell him about.

*May 4, 1976*

*It's been several weeks since my last surgery. Brandon has been so wonderful. He won't let me lift the laundry basket. He has been surprising me with breakfast in bed some mornings! I don't know what has gotten into him, but he makes me feel like a queen. I hope Bonnie was this good to him when he was recuperating from his accident. He wants me to get well so much that I don't have the heart to tell him I'm getting worse. I'm having a lot of trouble remembering. Sometimes I forget where I am when I'm in my very own bedroom.*

When October rolled around, Brandon's pink rosebush was still blooming profusely. It even did better as the weather cooled a bit. He carefully studied each bloom to determine which one would be judged the best. Brandon reminded Marilyn of the time they went to the fair together, and how she helped him judge the artwork. They laughed at the memory. She could remember things that happened a long time ago but not things that happened that morning.

Then Marilyn's condition got much worse. She really couldn't get out of bed. Her eyesight was failing rapidly. They never discussed the possibility that Marilyn was dying. Brandon wanted to pretend as long as he could. He brought cut roses in her bedroom. He opened the curtains wide to let every stream of sunlight in. He played beautiful music for her.

*October 10, 1976*

*Today I woke up and looked around my bedroom. I didn't recognize anything. I was afraid. I stayed in bed, closed my eyes, and waited. I don't know how long I waited before I started recognizing my surroundings. I can't tell Brandon.*

*October 13, 1976*

*Sometimes the words won't come. I want to say something, but the words won't come. I get so frustrated. Brandon said that it doesn't matter. I know it does.*

*October 22, 1976*

*Brandon brought a wheelchair home today. I'm not strong enough to walk. This way, he can get me into the kitchen, and I can sit and look out into the backyard. I like watching Brandon work in the yard. I'm getting weaker and weaker.*

*October 29, 1976*

*I can't think to write. I try, but it doesn't work. I'm*

*having trouble holding the pencil. I asked Bonnie to put my diary up. I won't be writing anymore.*

Gradually, Marilyn's eyesight diminished. Brandon suspected as much but never asked her about it. He could tell by how she followed sounds. Then one day when he thought she had lost the last bit of sight she had, Brandon spoke to her but then leaned far to the other side of the bed. She turned to where she heard the voice but never turned to where he actually was. Then he knew for sure. Shortly afterward, she lost her hearing. She heard nothing. She couldn't camouflage that disability. She couldn't fake her inability to hear so that Brandon wouldn't worry. Then gradually, it didn't matter anyway. Marilyn was there but ----she wasn't.

## Chapter Eighteen
## The Last Flight


Brandon woke up early one morning and glanced up at the wide, open sky. Fluffy, white clouds floated by peacefully in the giant sea of blue. The sky seemed to call out to Brandon. He had a very strong urge to fly through the open sky and leave all the problems back on the ground. Brandon made breakfast for Marilyn and then gave her a handful of pills. It was their usual morning routine----take all the pills.

It was a beautiful, spring morning. Brandon helped Marilyn into their car, and they headed to the small, private airport where he kept his plane. When they arrived, Brandon handed Marilyn another pill with a small cup of water. He helped her out of the car and into the plane where she waited while he went inside the office.

"Hey, Mr. Remington! Haven't seen you here in ages! I thought you'd forgotten how to fly! And that's your wife?" the maintenance worker asked as Brandon walked across the tarmac to the office. "Don't remember seeing her here before!"

"Yeah---we've been pretty busy and I'm getting on up there in years. I really shouldn't be flying with my little heart condition and all. We've decided to sell the plane, but my bride wanted to go up this last time. We'll only be up a few minutes. I want to show her that beautiful valley over there at the bottom of the mountain. It's so pretty this time of the year----be back in about 20 minutes."

With that, Brandon went out to the plane and climbed in. Marilyn was sitting in the next seat, as still as she could be. Her eyes were partially closed. She had never liked flying and never went on joy rides with Brandon, but she didn't really know where she was. As the plane climbed up to the appropriate altitude, Marilyn fell asleep. Brandon flew around in the sky, and for one minute he managed to forget-----loving every minute of the ride. For an instant, he forgot about everything. Then he glanced at Marilyn who seemed totally at peace. A tear trickled down his face.

*The crash of the plane echoed from the mountain to the valley below.*

2

The emergency vehicles raced to the scene of the accident. When the policeman questioned the witness to the crash, the witness said, "The airplane sounded just fine. It flew around, back and forth, and over the valley with no problem at all. Then, the plane dove straight into the mountain. The pilot must have had a heart attack or something. The engines sounded fine—no sign of distress or anything. The pilot didn't have his seatbelt on so he was thrown from the plane upon impact."

News traveled fast. One police officer rushed to locate Bonnie once he was told by the airport personnel who was flying the plane. The officer knocked on her door and stood there holding Brandon's wallet.

"Bonnie, I know how close you and your brother are. His plane crashed about 45 minutes ago. Brandon died in the crash, but he didn't suffer. I have his wallet and thought you should have it."

The minister pulled up to the front of the house just as the officer hugged Bonnie.

Bonnie took the wallet and held it next to her heart.

"Was his wife, Marilyn, with him?" Bonnie knew that she never went up in the airplane with Brandon. She hated flying--- particularly small, single-prop planes.

"Yes, she was. According to the man in the office, she wanted to go up for just one last time," the officer responded. "Can I do anything for you? Are you going to be alright by yourself here tonight?"

"Yes, I'm going to be OK," she said tearfully. A million things floated through her head. She said to herself again, *I'm going to be OK.*

Before the funeral, Bonnie opened Brandon's wallet, removed the brittle, aged piece of paper that he had carried for over 50 years and slipped it into

his hands.  She wanted him to be buried with it.
She was grief stricken but found only one consoling
fact---it was a blessing they went together.  Brandon
wanted it that way.  Bonnie knew that Brandon
would never leave Bonnie and would never live
without Bonnie.  Bonnie knew exactly what
happened.

Chapter Nineteen
Summersong Lane
January 8, 2006

"John!" Diane yelled from up in the attic. "Look what I found!" She was so excited. Diane had gone up in the attic to store their Christmas decorations. She saw a wooden box, smaller than a trunk, sitting back in the corner. When she opened the box, she found a very old, faded-red valentine box. Inside the box was a small diary. When Diane started reading, she couldn't stop. She realized she was reading about the former owners of the house. She sat mesmerized by the writing but a couple of entries were especially interesting to her.

John came to the foot of the ladder and with coaxing from Diane, climbed up into the attic where Diane was sitting.

Then she read another entry. "We were right! She is the one who liked to dance and remember the scuff marks on the living room floor when we first moved in? She used to dance around the room! Later when she got older and didn't dance anymore, they just carpeted over the scuff marks."

"Oh, my! Listen to this. OK---the writing tells about the stone vase! See? She put flowers in that vase to thank her husband for it----and, the pink rosebush! Her husband took care of that bush. It all makes sense now," she said excitedly.

"But they've been gone for over 20 years. Who did you see on the side of the house that day? What about the flowers in the vase and the trimmed rose bush? Are you saying there are ghosts here?" John questioned. "Are you saying these people have come back as ghosts or spirits?"

"I honestly don't know. I mean, I've never believed in ghosts before. I just know how meaningful these things were to the couple. This is proof of that. Isn't this wonderful?"

## Chapter Twenty
## Summersong Lane 2008

It is a beautiful, April morning. The Summersong house looks picture perfect in every way. The backyard is full of beautiful flowers and sculptured shrubbery. Cheerful birds and curious squirrels dance from tree to tree. Marilyn and Brandon are in the backyard, but they both appear much, much younger. They smile as they look around at the beautiful flowers and manicured lawn.

"Now look, darling! Look how beautifully these young people are taking care of the house. Lovely! Just lovely!" Marilyn said, looking twenty years younger and sounding very cheerful.

"Yes, they are," responded Brandon as he grabbed Marilyn around the waist and twirled her around, smiling and laughing.

Then Marilyn walked over to the rose bush near the back fence. She gently caressed a large rose in her hands and leaned down to smell its sweet fragrance.

"You love these pink roses, don't you, darling?" Marilyn asked.

"They've always been my favorite. Remember when I won the grand prize for these pink beauties?" Brandon beamed with pride as he recalled the memory.

"I knew you'd win. Everyone there said they were the most beautiful roses anyone had ever seen."

Brandon pulled off one of the smaller buds and placed it in Marilyn's hair. He kissed her gently. They turned to walk down the drive to the front of the house. As they passed the brick pillar, both glanced up at the stone vase Brandon cemented on top many, many years earlier. Marilyn gathered a few flowers and placed them in the vase.

Standing and looking at the front of the house from the sidewalk, they held each other.

"Isn't it beautiful?" Marilyn said looking proudly at the house they called home for almost twenty years.

"The most beautiful house I've ever seen."

"We had a wonderful life here, didn't we darling?"

"Our life couldn't have been better. You made me the happiest man alive each and every day."

Then in a very serious and melancholy tone, Marilyn whispered, "Brandon, are you ready to go now?"

Brandon glanced around the yard. "Yes, I think it's time to go."

Marilyn and Brandon walked spryly, actually skipping down the sidewalk in front of the house. About 20 feet down the sidewalk, they both broke into a dance, spinning and twirling. Laughter echoed through the trees overhead.

*Then their images.........*

*gradually faded..............*

*out of sight.*

The End

Made in the USA
Middletown, DE
20 July 2019